WRITING
THE BOOK OF
ESTHER

FRENCH EXPRESSIONS

HOLMES
&
MEIER

Julian Green, *Adrienne Mesurat*
Claude Roy, *The Distant Friend*
Anna Lorme, *A Traitor's Daughter*
Rabah Belamri, *Shattered Vision*
Henri Raczymow, *Writing the Book of Esther*
Alain Bosquet, *A Russian Mother*

WRITING THE BOOK OF ESTHER

HENRI RACZYMOW

TRANSLATED FROM THE FRENCH
BY DORI KATZ

HM

HOLMES & MEIER

NEW YORK / LONDON

Published in the United States of America 1995 by
Holmes & Meier Publishers, Inc.
160 Broadway
New York, NY 10038

Originally published in French as *Un Cri Sans Voix*,
© Éditions Gallimard, 1985

Book design by Miriam Schaer

This book has been printed on acid-free paper.

Library of Congress Cataloging-in-Publication Data

Raczymow, Henri, 1948–
   [Cri sans voix.   English]
   Writing the Book of Esther / Henri Raczymow ; translated by Dori
Katz.
     p.   cm.—(French expressions series)
   ISBN 0-8419-1335-8
   1. Children of Holocaust survivors—France—History—Fiction.
2. Jews—France—History—20th century—Fiction I. Katz, Dori.
II. Title. III. Series.
PQ2678.A245C7513   1995
843′.914—dc20   94-37604
                                              CIP

Manufactured in the United States of America

---

*I would like to thank here my aunt and
uncles—Fanny Grouman, Charles Rapoport,
Noich Oksenberg—as well as my father, for
their testimony.*

For a long time I thought that I was born and that I died on June 22, 1944. . . . I was not old enough to fight, but as soon as I saw the light of day, I was old enough to have been killed in the crematoria of Poland.

Pierre Goldman

WRITING
THE BOOK OF
ESTHER

My older sister, Esther, died on a spring day, in the spring of 1975. Her disappearance caused us no grief, at least not that you could tell. To us that event was the rotten fruit of the fatality we were caught in and could, by definition, do nothing about. We had noticed the daily deterioration of that fruit on the family tree; we expected it to fall because we knew that, sooner or later, it was bound to happen. In truth, Esther's suicide was almost a relief. It elicited no comment from us, even less regret. She had become completely identified with the "sickness" we thought she suffered, and although we didn't know the name of this "sickness," as far as we were concerned it was incurable. We didn't speak about it. It was a little as if by her suicide she had sacrificed herself for us, so that we might live. We almost should have thanked her. But obviously that was not why she had done it, so that we might live. And we wanted to live—live out, no matter how short, the time allotted to us. So life went on. Eventually, the concentric circles on the even and liquid surface of time became smaller and smaller every day and finally blurred. It was more than forgetfulness: nothing had happened. Our silence, as far as Esther was concerned, was not a deliberate intent not to remember her. Our silence was not a substitute for words about guilt, or remorse, or nostalgia. Especially not nostalgia. On the contrary, our silence seemed so effortless, so natural, that it was as if Esther had really never existed. Never existed except in dreams, or rather in nightmares, but the kind of hazy, fuzzy nightmares that disappear on awakening, leaving nothing behind except a sort of vague uneasiness, very vague.

We knew how to pay our last respects to her. The hole was plugged, the wound closed, the rotten fruit returned to the earth. We had followed tradition, had seen to it that her burial in the Bagneux cemetery went according to the appropriate ritual. Now we were even.

But one day the dead woman resurfaced. It was in the summer of 1982. That summer the Israeli defense army invaded southern Lebanon, engaged the Palestinian army in a merciless battle, and occupied West Beirut. The campaign was called "Peace in Galilee." Shortly afterward, the newspapers informed us that "Peace in Galilee" meant "a genocide unprecedented in the history of mankind." We also learned that West Beirut was the exact replica of the Warsaw Ghetto. In the fall, however, the newspapers said that they had been slightly mistaken. There had been no genocide. And West Beirut had no connection to the Warsaw Ghetto between 1940 and 1943. None whatsoever. So sorry.

That summer, and that summer only, I remembered that in a very distant and very near past, seven years ago, I had a sister, Esther, who killed herself, by gas, at the age of thirty-two. I hardly knew her. But when I thought of her, what I saw were images of the Warsaw Ghetto, where with her ridiculous and oversized cap she stood out, a slim silhouette against the background of a city I did not know, a city that would soon become a field of ruins. For me, Esther was a little like this city. Because of the cap. She had unearthed it God knows where and wore it the same way the young Jewish women fighters wore theirs in a photo displayed then, as it is still today, on a wall of her room. When I was little, I knew nothing about these women fighters. I didn't think about them, just as later, when Esther died, I didn't think about the reasons for her act. In truth, her suicide didn't raise questions in my mind, nor did it puzzle me. Like those things that are so obvious it doesn't occur to you to question them. They had to happen. Period. For me it was somewhat like the fate of the Warsaw Jews. And all the Jews of Poland. And of all of Europe. Why did the Nazis want to exterminate them all? I mean, to what advantage?

Four events occurred in the months preceding her death that should be noted: her trip to New York during the summer, her separation from her husband, Simon P, her resignation from teaching, her falling head over heels for a filmmaker, a certain Jacques Lipshitz. Trip, separation, resignation, love—all these seemed more like signals than reasons.

It isn't that we couldn't explain her action, nor that we knew too little about Esther. No, the reason for her act was almost too patent, too clear: Esther was "sick," and the cause of her "sickness" was the war. Yet, Esther didn't know the war. She was born in France, during the German occupation, on August 2, 1943. When she learned later that this was the precise date of the rebellion in the death camp at Treblinka, she must have said

3

to herself: "I was born on August 2, 1943, in France. But it's in Treblinka that I would have liked to die, that day, that I should have died."

Born during the war, she had never left the war. Born in France, she lived nevertheless in Warsaw, on Nowolipie Street where Daddy had lived before he came to France. For her, no doubt, that particular war should have swallowed everything in its wake, and should never have had an afterward, of whatever shape or form. But there had been an afterward. Our life, that was an afterward. What choice did we have?

Seven years after her death, on a summer night in 1982, Esther, my sister, came alive again in my writing, but with character traits different from those belonging to the girl whose life bordered, but only bordered, on mine for years, traits of a character she perhaps dreamed about and one she impersonated, a girl who was twenty years old in 1940. Like one of the women in the photograph.

The pages I wrote that evening were not a posthumous homage to my sister. Rather they were a summons for me to experience what I believed she had lived through in spirit—the extermination of the European Jews by the Nazis. I fell prey to a similar obsession, although I didn't know it yet. On a summer day, in 1982, I discovered all at once that I had had a sister, a sister who had committed suicide by putting her head in the oven, and that this sister, this ghost, was the surrogate of other ghosts. Ghosts who, at the very moment that Esther was born, were identified by the striped pajamas that hung on their barbed-wire bodies.

I

Affliction was their second
nature, and the vocabulary of
their heart was reduced to one
word: OY

Abraham J. Heschel

It is probably a sign of nervousness: Esther "entertains herself" by repeatedly drawing oval ovals, always the same handsome oval that turns into the outline of a face. At the top of the oval, the line goes back on itself and, instead of closing the circle, enters it with a curl that looks like an apostrophe. She draws a very small rectangle in the lower part of the oval. Then, almost as if in a daze, she judges the result. She likes it because it seems rather obvious. To make it even more so, she blackens the little rectangle . . .

By now, she has drawn dozens of these faces, all identical, fascinating. What's especially fascinating is not so much the face itself (although . . .), but the ease with which she's able to arrive at a perfect resemblance. As with all who don't "know" how to draw, likeness is the main point: she is amazed that these so simple, so elementary lines do indeed form a face, and precisely that particular face, his, yes his, that of A. H. She almost forgets who A. H. is, so set is she on capturing the likeness, almost as if it were traced. But she gets hold of herself: "I'm getting distracted . . ."

In time, with this drawing repeated endlessly on sheets of paper piling up, Esther is proud of herself. But she's wrong—she knows that she didn't invent these features. She simply saw this drawing yesterday, on a wall, on Mylna Street. Or was it Leszno Street? No, Mylna Street. It had been crossed out.

While Esther is drawing or writing (for she also writes, that is, tries her hand at poetry—oh, she's already filled a fat notebook—or at meditations, diaries that she abandons, then takes up again after long intervals. Sometimes, she's even struck by the crazy notion that she'll become a writer, later), she's constantly disturbed by the sound of furniture being hoisted, dragged about. People move in, people move out. But Esther is there for no one. Is any of this her concern? Her parents, her brother, see to everything. She has earned this withdrawal, sitting at her table, in front of the *Tennis Player*, Uncle Nathan's sculpture. He refused to have it shown at the Olympic Games in Berlin as the Art Committee of Warsaw wanted to do. Perhaps it would have brought him fame, but principles count for something, don't they?

Thank God that the Litvaks aren't budging; they won't leave Nowolipie. What a crazy idea to go live in the suburbs of Praga, like this young couple related to Adek. They are Esther's cousins but she hardly knows them, doesn't know them at all. They're going to occupy the apartment above, left vacant by the Poles who are leaving. Esther isn't at all impatient to see them, to make their acquaintance. There's plenty of time. And then, she believes, they're simple people. Chaim Litvak is a shoemaker. He's very pious, not like Adek. Between shoes to be resoled and his prayerbook, where does he find time for *real* books? As for Guta, the wife, Esther has no opinion, she'll see, judge on the evidence.

No matter what she says (and she says plenty), since the beginning of the war Esther hasn't been able to fix her attention on a book, no matter how interesting. She much prefers daydreaming over these ovals with their curls and their blackened rectangle in the center. An obsession. As soon as she's seated at her table, after greeting the *Tennis Player* with a ritualistic and perhaps exorcising *shalom*, she grabs her pencil and draws A. H. Sometimes she turns around quickly, thinking that Adek or Freydla are looking over her shoulder. But invariably she's wrong. Or perhaps it's Mathiek. No, she is really alone. They're all too busy helping the cousins from Praga. The noise they make is unbearable. She misses little Zofia and her mazurkas. Shoemakers don't play mazurkas; they play the hammer, that's all.

You would think that typhus and lice are less a concern to the Poles than to us. A. H. says so. As for the Germans—hardened, tanned, invulnerable—they don't care one bit about lice or typhus. By dint of repeating "hard as Krupp steel, hard as Krupp steel," they have become steel. And what power do lice have over steel, over Krupp which is more than steel? The Poles are already more susceptible to typhus. But, my God, what fragility! They're like newborn babies, running the greatest risks. The least little louse, and it's typhus. That explains our quarantine. It must be for our own good. And for what else could it be? How many are we at this very minute to benefit from this quarantine? Three hundred, four hundred thousand? And all huddled together, in the same streets. It's an endless merry-go-round: the Poles leave and the Jews arrive. It's a madhouse and, one floor up, I'll no longer be able to listen to Zofia's waltzes and quadrilles. Let the Jews be happy—finally they're among their own kind. With the lice. And what are lice like? Esther has never seen any, at least not that she remembers. She'll ask Szymon to give her a "lecture" on the subject. There's nothing he doesn't know.

Szymon Pessakowicz, Esther saw him again this morning. In truth, he didn't look any more handsome than on previous days, but she's convinced that he would throw himself in the water for her—plash, in the Vistula, an ice-cold bath. As for the Vistula, it'll be a long day before they see that river again. Esther doesn't care. All that she asks for is that she be left alone to write. She feels she's impossible to live with. But at least she's honest with herself. She's very well aware that she has her faults. Has she ever denied it? This is one of her great qualities: she is honest with herself and with others. What does she ask for herself? Nothing more than to be left in peace. So, why should they ask more of her than she asks of them?

What bothers Esther the most about Szymon is that his learning is exclusively scientific. He knows an infinite number of things about the greatest variety of subjects but he knows nothing about literature. Neither Polish, Russian, Yiddish nor Hebrew literature. Or at least not much. When he was little he knew Hebrew but he must have forgotten it when he went to a Polish high school. His ambition—to get the Nobel Prize in Biology. How ridiculous. My ambition, as I've told him many times— to become a writer. Esther and Szymon spend time comparing their mutual ambitions without either one of them convincing the other. These discussions go nowhere, and afterward, look who's sulking. Even if they still hold hands. Esther recognizes their childishness, especially hers. All in all, she would be very proud if Szymon were to get the Nobel Prize, even in biology. I wouldn't hesitate to marry a man with a Nobel Prize. If he insisted, of course.

Once more, Esther should have approved of Szymon's idea: to leave for France, or England. Better yet, *for America*. Both of us have relatives there. If he stays in Poland, Szymon has no chance of getting a Nobel Prize. Unless perhaps he converts. Esther makes a face: one must keep what is left of Jewishness, already we're speaking less and less Yiddish, more and more Polish. Rumors have it that even those who converted will be forced to live in the Jewish Quarter. A lot of good it did them! That'll teach them. For them, it must be even worse of a nightmare than it is for everyone else, those who thought nothing of betraying their ancestors for the sake of what they hoped would be a better life. Now here is calamity catching up with them, routing them from the very haven of their churches, churches for converts, disparaged churches. Calamity is a clever bloodhound. A Sherlock Holmes without peer. As for us, we who keep "the old house," calamity is no stranger. Not once through the ages has it spared us. We'll be faithful to it until death— or, as they say, until the Messiah comes. Others pretend that the Angel of Death will precede the coming of the Messiah; that this century will witness the greatest calamity in our history. These petty prophets. These yeshiva Cassandras with their unverifiable, inconsistent, messianic reckonings.

I would have liked to be capable of writing a novel, a real novel. As good as Elisza Orszeszkowa, at least as good but more artful. But how can you think of art in an upside-down world, where at any moment you could be killed? Most of the windows in the houses of Warsaw have been blown to bits: they've been repaired any which way. People whose homes were bombed wander the roads in

11

the greatest confusion. Some are leaving Warsaw, others come here to find refuge; it's hard to know what to do now. The Litvaks decided to remain on Nowolipie Street and Esther to keep this journal. Oh, it won't be a work of art, far from it, but while waiting for A. H.'s death, I mean waiting for him to be killed (the French or the English will soon succeed) one must be especially careful not to lose the habit of writing. Then, when peace returns, she'll start a novel, a real one. She'll be mature. These events will have matured her. Every cloud has its silver lining. This selfish-to-the-point-of-abasement disposition is, she thinks, the signature of her artistic nature. Oh, she was looking for proof and here it is. The writer is the one who does not fear words. And this will be my last thought for the day.

O

There was a meeting, Grzybowska Street, in front of the community center. Adek went. Zionists and Bundists bickered, as usual, and each speaker, no matter what he said, was booed by half the audience; never the same half—that would have been too simple. It's always like that with Jews. As Adek says: "Two Jews, three opinions," or "two Jews, one party; three Jews, a secession." The question was how to find a way to refuse the Germans' orders to bring five thousand more people into the Jewish Quarter. Answer: so many bags of zlotys.

Moving stories. Months before the invasion, Adek and Freydla had planned to leave the Jewish Quarter. Adek had gotten wind of a beautiful shop up for grabs, and all of us went to see it. Esther, apparently with time on her hands that day, had let herself be dragged along on this ridiculous and vulgar expedition. It was a sinister scene:

her father walking back and forth on the premises as if he already owned the place, chanting numbers with an exalted air; her mother talking dress with the shop lady while Mathiek was nosing around in all corners inspecting God knows what. Once home, all three discussed the project: Mathiek added fuel to the conversation, wondering precisely how much money they would have to borrow. What an abyss between Esther and these three creatures! That's it, that's how she thought of them, three creatures. She, on the other hand, took after Uncle Avrum. If, like him, she had no business sense, that's because, like him, she disdained "business" things. And Mathiek, exactly her father in miniature.

As soon as Jews start making money, their great idea is to assimilate with the Poles. They're ashamed to speak Yiddish. They change their names. They send their children to Polish schools. Sometimes they go as far as to convert. But first they have to move. Tell me where you are living, and I'll tell you who you are and what kind of Jew you are and what kind of Jew you no longer are. Today, there's no longer a question of moving. On the contrary. Szymon's family had to return to our neighborhood after having left some years ago. Szymon will have to interrupt his studies. Already his Polish university friends turn their back on him, and he's hurt by it, dejected. To come back here, to Krochmalna Street, seems to him, in his slightly presumptuous terms, a "social and psychological regression." "It's not as if I looked Jewish," he always says. Which is unbearable for Esther. And me, do I look Jewish? With a smile of commiseration, Szymon says that yes. It's as if he said: "Poor kid, you're sick, it's obvious, your face is covered with a rash." This deep-seated self-hatred. As Esther sees it, people like the Pessakowiczes spend the best part of their time striving to scratch the pimples off their faces. Some of them succeed, but the pimples don't really disappear; they lie buried beneath the skin, ready to erupt at the slightest provocation.

First of all, Esther hates moving. That's because they lived in so many places since she was born. Let's see, in chronological order, it was Mylna Street first. Then Nowolipki. Then Nalewki. Then Bonifraterska. And finally Nowolipie, end of the line. From now on, if she ever moves again it will be to Paris, London, or New York. With or without Szymon. And second . . . no, no second. That's it.

O

Szymon's father was the most upset by the Pessako-wiczes' return to the neighborhood. So much effort for nothing, he must have told himself. But Adek was no less upset by the rumors in the street. When the creation of a quarantine area in the quarter was announced, he came running home, breathless, and told his wife that they were leaving, now, right away, that he was gathering all his money and that they were going to Cracow, Lodz, Lublin, Vilna—I don't know where. "Will you look at this *mishugene*, this wild golem," asked Freydla, "where is he running off to?" And her reaction calmed him down a little. Perhaps the Germans would change their mind. Perhaps the Jewish Council could cajole them, with a little money, of course. "But who's not paying! I'm ready to pay! We're all ready to pay! We are already paying, drop it." Adek was screaming in the living room, pacing back and forth. A madman. Then Freydla reminded him that he had managed to find a *modus vivendi* with the provisional German administrator assigned to his store.

This opportune remark was just about to calm him when Mathiek, sadistically or perhaps unconsciously, asked him if provisional didn't in this case mean permanent, and if it wasn't rather he, Adek, who was there provisionally? Flabbergasted, Adek stared at his son for a long time without moving. Then, not saying another word, he left the living room. I'm afraid that, for once, Mathiek had shown himself to be completely lucid. That evening, he told me to hope that Papa would get along well with that German. It could come in handy later, or rather sooner, than we thought. Was he joking? Alas, no.

○

Szymon got in touch with the *Hashomer Hatzair*, a Zionist youth movement. Esther has a hard time admitting that Szymon takes any action at all without warning her, without consulting her. He tells her, of course, that's the least he can do, but after the fact. Perhaps that's how he'll some day tell her that he loves another woman. Absolutely unthinkable. First of all, it's Szymon who is in love with Esther. She likes him a lot, and why not? How could one help but like Szymon? He's nice, he's smart. But there's nothing in him to get passionate about, nothing intoxicating, exalting to the pitch of fever. All in all, his great virtue is to be in love with Esther. That's not much. He's the kind of young man a girl's parents will like, thinking above all of their daughter's happiness. Rather, not her happiness but her security. For Szymon gives the impression of being a serious young man, responsible, having his feet on the ground. All this doesn't add up to enough for Esther: Is that all she can hope for? Security? And what of her work, then?

Szymon's return to Judaism surprised and rather

pleased Adek. But he didn't hide his reservations about the young man's political choices. Jews, said Adek, must make their revolution right where they live, with the other workers, not in the Negev or the Galilee. Daddy got a little heated up, confronting again the old controversies of his youth. But now he recites these slogans mechanically, insincerely. It's a game. Szymon has a hard time confronting him. He doesn't like to play games, just the opposite of Daddy. Because you must have a sense of play to talk politics—play and futility. Come to think of it, this is Szymon's great flaw: the lack in him of all sense of play. He is serious down to his bones.

O

Esther has the feeling that soon they'll no longer be able to leave the ghetto. This means that the Jewish Quarter, let's say from Muranowska until Zlota Street, will become a real ghetto. And there are so many places in Warsaw that Esther hardly knows. Praga, for example, where the Pessakowiczes come from, and Freydla's relatives, and the Tenenbaums, and Adek's cousins. Why not take the streetcar and go for a walk there, cross the Vistula while there's still time? That's what Esther asks herself every night. But the next morning she gives it up because of a deep, inexplicable fear that she cannot deny. What if, while she was wandering away from the quarter, the Germans built an unbreachable wall and cut her off from her parents forever, and from Mathiek, from Yanek, and from Szymon too? When Esther was small she had such nightmares. She used to wake up in the middle of the night screaming, and go to Mathiek and wake him as well. What a pest she was! Please God, see to it that these frightening fantasies don't become realities. It's true that today she could always go to Krochmalna Street and wake up Szymon. He would reassure her, he would, and she could slip into his bed, press against him, put her head on his chest, and he would stroke her hair, and she would fall back asleep. But what if he himself were caught in the same nightmare? What if we're all cracking up? No help anywhere then. Not even, I fear, in this journal.

O

It's snowing. Wearing the star of David on their arms, Charles and his cousin Chaim went to line up on Grzybowska Street to register for labor camp. Speak of humiliation!

Evening. In the end, Charles was exempt thanks to the intervention of his "provisional administrator." The *Judenrat* clerk simply sent him home: his official exemption notice was stamped in the register, countersigned by a secretary of the Jewish Council. Someone must have paid a pretty sum of zlotys for that. Besides, it's perfectly legal to buy an exemption. It costs a thousand zlotys. Chaim couldn't get the money. Adek couldn't help him. He didn't exactly say "it's not my problem," but that's what he meant. In any case, it isn't mine either, believe me.

Adek reported that while waiting in line, the Jews talked of politics. Communists, Bundists, Zionists, religious fanatics, all of them gossiped, traded insults, slandered each other, trying to outdo each other in snatching the latest rumor. What a family we are! The whole gamut of the political rainbow, from the left of left to the right of right, and every shade of religious practice, from the most Orthodox of the Orthodox to the most exalted of

17

the Hasidim, and all the hues of assimilation—converts, Polish-speaking patriots, half-Jews, quarter-Jews, Poles of "Moses' persuasion," or "of Jewish origin." They all hate each other and spied on each other. Like a family! I fear that this infinite palette of shimmering hues will blend into a uniform gray, totally. Then, the time will have come. A. H. said so. Already, we all wear the same star of David. Well, almost the same. Those who can afford it wear one made of cloth (three zlotys), the others wear a paper one (fifty groszy). Just like with the dead—a rich man's funeral and a poor man's funeral. But in the end, but in the end?

With all these refugees arriving, there will soon be four hundred thousand of us in the quarter. "They're cheek by jowl," our Polish "brothers" will go on to say. Esther understands Szymon's disenchantment as far as those "brothers" are concerned. Poor Szymon who doesn't even look Jewish. To treat him like this, to dare treat him like this, as if he had the plague. To see them change so quickly, so absolutely. According to Esther, they haven't changed, they were always like that. It's simply that the arrival of the Germans in their tanks, with their theories of *Über-* and *Untermenschen*, gives "our brothers" permission to say out loud what they've been thinking to themselves, and for the worst of them, to act out what they proclaim. Now, for them, it's a question of discovering a grandmother of German origin. Yes, the ideal is to be *Volksdeutsch*, a Pole of German extraction. Esther, shamelessly selfish, sees at least two advantages in what's happening to Szymon. First of all, he's returning to Judaism even if it's only by belonging to a Zionist-Socialist youth movement. Second, he'll stop eyeing the Polish girls who are more liberated than us, that is, easier. Esther still hasn't "granted" Szymon anything.

But I want him to be available, right then and there, when I think the moment is ripe. Perhaps he's already been with a Polish girl. It doesn't matter. Papa often said that a boy, even a good Jewish boy, can keep company with a Polish girl. For fun. Adek himself, when he was young, went with Polish girls, and he never hid it from Momma, nor from us because to him it seemed so pardonable, so matter of fact, so conforming to the most banal and inevitable *Bildungsroman* plot that the most average young Jewish man must live out. But he always adds that he married a real Jewish girl, and, in the end, that's what matters.

O

Impossible to have contact with the outside now. You can't send out news anymore or receive money. Typhus is wreaking its havoc. We no longer have the right to go out between nine o'clock at night and five in the morning. For disobeying this decree, the Litvaks' family doctor, Dr. Finkiel, was killed, even though he had a pass. Szymon reports that at the headquarters of *Hashomer Hatzair*, on Leszno Street, refugees keep warm by burning library books. People are being held for ransom even in their own homes; the extortioners can be Germans (from the *Wehrmacht* or from the SS, "the skull and crossbones" division), *Volksdeutsche*, or simply Poles. Adek says that the Jews have once again become Pharaoh's slaves: they won't build pyramids this time, rather great projects for the new Egypt. His cousin Chaim has a different opinion. He says that it's impossible to compare Ramses to A. H. The former is an angel next to the latter, who is no less than the Angel of Death. But from this particular Egypt, he says, there will be no exit for the

Jews. Even Ha-Shem, our God, won't be able to get them out.

There is still time to leave—for example, to Palestine. It seems that it's possible, expensive but possible. What are we waiting for? On Nowolipki Street, the Germans are ransacking the apartments of rich Jews, especially those who were lawyers. They've created a ghetto in Lodz. All the Jews from the region were transferred there empty-handed, and had to rely on their own wits to find a place to live. Thousands of Jews are concentrated in Lublin. For what purpose? Esther has stopped drawing A. H.'s face. It no longer amuses her, not in the least. She doesn't think about a novel either. She doesn't think about anything anymore.

O

Prisoners of war came back to Poland, among them some Jews. Six hundred of them were repatriated to Lublin, then sent to Parczew. Why, I don't know. Thirteen soldiers accompanied them and killed them on the way. They let themselves be killed without a fight. When the survivors were questioned, they said that, yes indeed, they could have fought, but they didn't because they thought it would have been bad for the Jews. BECAUSE IT WOULD HAVE BEEN BAD FOR THE JEWS! Here you have the Jewish mentality! Let's allow ourselves to be killed—if not, it will be bad for the Jews. This is the kind of joke, a *witz*, that would have amused Doctor Freud, before the war. Alas.

Adek got a job on the snow-plowing crew and thanks to certain mysterious connections—zlotys or, rather dollars—had Szymon and Mathiek hired, too. For days now, Esther has been seeing the Lipshitzes regularly. Jacob is a poet. At least, that's what people say because Jacob himself doesn't make a big deal about it. Besides, he doesn't speak much about himself. Perhaps Esther's presence intimidates him. Perhaps by his very silence he is trying to tell her something. She's noticed that before speaking—she herself doesn't take her eyes off him—he lifts his head and looks at her first. Yes, he must be shy. If he hardly speaks in public, it's because he thinks that what he has to say isn't worthwhile, but he's wrong. Unless, and this is what Esther is inclined to believe, he thinks his audience unworthy. The same holds true for his poetry. He has such an intelligent look. He is tall. He is blond. The only flaw I see in him is that his hair is thinning, but that's such a minor flaw. Then perhaps also a slight tendency toward plumpness, though offset by his height. How old could he be? Perhaps forty, but barely. His wife Helena is insignificant. (I'll never understand what grotesque chance brings people together.) She is the "Aryan" type, as Szymon would say, blond with blue eyes. When she was little, her parents called her *shiksele*, little *goye*. Helena has a fancy for literature—Yiddish, Russian, and Polish. She holds soirees where they read poetry—but never Jacob's. Her daughter Martha is like her in personality, but she's a curly-haired brunette. She plays Chopin and Liszt beautifully, and when she's at the piano Jacob seems in ecstasy. So am I when I look at him listening to his daughter. I hope I don't show it. Helena looks the same way, but I don't know, on her everything looks ridiculous. She's a superficial woman, totally pre-occupied with appearances. Day after day, Esther wonders if Jacob's really in love with Helena, if he ever was. What a mismatched couple, too ill-suited to last for long.

It's interesting how, right away, Szymon hated Jacob and exaggerated Helena's good points. What good points?

Her elegance? Her taste in literature? Her skills as a hostess? He doesn't see, through this veneer, her genuine and deep lack of culture, her vulgarity. As for his aversion to Jacob, there's a good reason for it—pure and simple jealousy. Of course, he won't admit it. He'll argue, rationalize, but in doing so gives himself away by denying the obvious—Jacob's irresistible charm and his own jealousy. Esther is very aware of it: Szymon really suffers during these evenings at the Lipshitzes'. He seems more and more reluctant to attend and gives all sorts of excuses to beg off: he's tired, or he has some pressing work to read for his doctoral thesis, or whatever. If he at all bothers to come to Jacob and Helena's, it's because Esther insists, and he can't refuse her anything. He is obedient. He'll avoid her eyes, lower his head and murmur, "okay, I'll go." Esther smiles at his kindness but also at his sadness. In the Lipshitzes's living room, he doesn't say a word, looks sullen, gives out incoherent rumblings when people are clumsy enough to ask him what's wrong. Esther, sitting next to him on the green velvet armchair, sometimes will lean over and whisper, "try."

For Esther, Szymon is like a big brother. Or a kid brother, even though he's bigger and older than her. But there's no maternal instinct in this feeling that he's her "kid brother"—she's completely free of such instincts. Why then? Is it some disturbing and obscure desire to regard him from the least virile perspective, to feminize him—in other words, to dominate him, or to prevent him from dominating her? But part of it is also her awareness of a real similarity between them. From the bottom of their hearts they share a feeling of disdain for themselves and others, a disdain linked to an immense pride. They're really chips off the same block. They even resemble each other physically. People who don't know them think they're brother and sister the first time they see them together. They love being alike; they love each other because they are alike. Because it's easy. But it might be that a part of themselves aspires to something else. For Esther, this something else would come under the guise of Jacob Lipshitz. He at last would dominate her. It's impossible to think of Jacob as a kid brother. Maybe like her father. Like Adek, yes, like Adek in the bygone days when she admired her father, when he was everything to her, when she was in love with him.

O

Jacob Lipshitz started a Jewish self-defense group, mostly to fight young Polish hoodlums from the business school who attacked Jewish merchants on Leszno Street. These thugs go into stores and wreck the merchandise. On the way they attack Jews, singling out the Hasidim, whose caftans they rip and whose beards they pull until they come off.

Adek says that the Poles *are born* anti-Semites. While still a fetus in their mother's belly they're already anti-Semites. Which isn't the case with Germans, he says, who are simply conditioned by A. H. and his propaganda; anti-Semitism is not innate in them. . . . What Papa's comments reveal is the Jews' ineradicable love for the Germans, for German culture and language. How many of us thought that Germany wouldn't harm us when it attacked Poland because the German people are like our brothers? The proof is that they *almost* speak our language. Yet Franz Kafka established once and for all that there was a bottomless gulf between German and Yiddish. Who among us would call his mother *Mutter*, Kafka asked? Uncle Avrum often said, When the Jews left Egypt and were at last free in the desert they began to miss the land of their enslavement. This confirms what needs no confirmation, the despicable love of the slave for his master. As for me, I would like to be Jacob's slave; I sense that he has a masterful soul with something of the German, of the Pharaoh, in him. In his youth, I believe, he was a student at the university in Berlin. To dare to be despicable, to dare what others wouldn't dare. Once in a while, only once in a while . . . Esther is disgusted with herself. Deeply disgusted. She doesn't deserve to live. She thought about it recently. As she sees it, certain people, because of their very nature, have earned the right to live, *ipso facto*. For example, her brother Mathiek. His good disposition, his simple love of life earn him, naturally, the right to live. Others aren't worthy of this verb: to earn. No, they have not earned it. Because they don't love life. They are not worthy of life. Esther is not worthy of life. She hasn't earned it. She is disgusted with herself.

O

In the end, Mathiek signed on with the battalion of masons that Jacob Lipshitz now has also joined. They earn half a zloty per day removing bricks from bombed houses and loading them in wheelbarrows. Jacob is teaching Mathiek the art of working as slowly as possible to save his strength. There are many intellectuals among these laborers, perhaps only one real mason per hundred. They work on Franciszkanska, Nalewki, Bonifraterska streets. Adek and his cousin Chaim have joined up with a group of construction workers. They had the task yesterday of piling up huge quantities of bricks along Bonifraterska Street. What are the Germans' real intentions, they wondered. To build a wall, Jacob thinks.

Raids in the street are becoming more frequent. At the head of the police is a motorcyclist who calls out, "Jews! Stop." And the Jews stop, glued to the spot; then they're arrested and taken away by truck.

Adek told me how before the war, in the days preceding the first of May, the police would come to the homes of people suspected of being Communists and arrest them so that they couldn't participate in subversive demonstrations. They were released on May 2. This happened every year to Bolek, Daddy's brother. He would come home with a beard. Same time next year, he would be arrested again.

Last night, at the Lipshitzes' home, we told funny stories, an occurrence rare enough for Esther to make note of it. Szymon and Jacob competed in liveliness. She hadn't laughed this hard in months. She laughed so hard that she was crying as she lost her balance and fell against Szymon like a rag doll. Home in her room, around midnight, she realized that she'd been the prize of a tournament between two knights full of desire for her. No, she doesn't think she's mistaken. Getting undressed for bed, slowly, almost voluptuously, she smiled at her herself repeatedly in the mirror she tried to avoid. But her gaze kept returning to it. It was beyond her, and she smiled and smiled at herself because she found herself pretty. Surely, she told herself, both Szymon and Jacob must have noticed how pretty she was tonight, both wanted to conquer her and hated the other as a rival, and none of this, come to think of it, was unpleasant. Poor Helena also laughed, the fool, not noticing what was happening.

"What? A Jew with no armband?" screamed A. H. upon seeing Jesus during a trip to paradise.

"Don't insist," replied Saint Peter, "it's the boss's son."

Jacob told this joke that was going around Warsaw.

In order to survive, Jews are capable of the greatest prowess. This "greatest prowess" sometimes takes the form of great compromises. Just how far can one go to survive at any cost? They say that the *Judenrat* in Cracow collaborates with the deportations. They must have their reasons, good reasons probably. But.

To survive at any cost: the novelty of our situation lies precisely in these words loaded with contradiction. To survive? At any cost? How can one ignore that it's precisely at the cost of death, perhaps the death of others, for the time being? But the death of others is only a prelude to our own. If what they say about the *Judenrat* of Cracow proves true, then Jews are surviving there at the cost of other Jews. Some day we in Warsaw will be in the same boat, perhaps some day soon.

O

Every building has its designated "committee." Ours, 42 Nowolipie Street, consists of Jacob Lipshitz, Guta Litvak, Reb Huberband—a rabbi elected president of the committee—and Esther. They met at the home of Chaim and Guta Litvak. Everyone had the chance to voice his or her recriminations, or suggestions for improving cleanliness and undertaking certain repairs. Esther also had the opportunity to get better acquainted with cousin Guta. Guta, incredibly, had begun medical school at the University of Warsaw but dropped out to marry Chaim. It's scandalous. What an extraordinary difference between them. Guta is a committed Zionist. She joined a pioneering farm in Grochow, in a suburb of Warsaw, where they train you to go live in Palestine. When Reb Huberband gave her the floor, she criticized the petty complaints of the other tenants, saying they had more urgent tasks to accomplish. First of all, she said, we should institute a clandestine school. Second, organize a youth club. Third and fourth, I don't remember. Guta is a militant with a positive attitude. Esther admires her on the one hand, but, on the other, she doesn't. She hates the "positive" attitude trapped in material things.

Next Jacob spoke, and to Esther's great surprise, suggested her as "director" of the school. There are about twenty children of school age in the building. Their parents could take turns providing a room in their apartment for class. Everybody agreed with Jacob's suggestion. Esther will try to rise to the occasion. But why did she accept, and what's more, with gratitude? Is she in the process of betraying her own values? Has she, in her heart of hearts, already given up being a writer? But this is no small matter, kiddo!

O

The worst of it is that she's happy, and this happiness makes her lose sleep. She thinks of her mission constantly, what a mess. Schoolmistress! In spite of everything, it's better than selling hats like Adek. No, not at all, it's the same. No difference. Except for Art, everything is the same. Selling hats, teaching, building bridges, making babies, falling in love, yes, even falling in love. No hierarchies. The rest, it's to keep busy. And if possible, to gratify yourself. Why not? Self-gratification doesn't contribute anything but show me how it hinders Art. With her new responsibility, Esther feels as though she's getting even, but doesn't know with whom or what. It's ridiculous, isn't it. But the fact remains that Papa is also very proud. "Now that you're really a *mensch* . . ." Esther beams in front of her mirror at the idea that Papa is proud of her. Adek hasn't been her prince for a long time, but some vestiges of his former splendor still remain. Adek, Jacob, Szymon, at least three men admire her now. "Her" three men. They belong to her. She belongs to them. Not another word.

She went looking for Hannah Krawetz, a friend of Helena Lipshitz. Before the German invasion, Hannah taught at the Jewish school on Okopowa Street. Yanek, Esther's little brother, knows her by sight though she wasn't his teacher. She accepted with enthusiasm Esther's offer to teach at the Nowolipie Street School. Hannah's school had closed down, and she misses her young pupils. Esther questioned her little brother to get his reaction: Yanek would be delighted to go to school in his own home. Reb Huberband already promised to transmit the words of our wise men to the children, and Martha Lipshitz will initiate them into the joys of music. . . . Into what madness have I ventured? And my writing? Do I really want to be a writer or was it only an adolescent fantasy? But what matters in life except that? Responsibilities? Honors? Pleasing my men? Making a few women jealous—Momma, Helena? What petty ambition, little frog.

Behind Esther's back, dissension is already brewing. According to Jacob, Guta Litvak and the rabbi came to a violent confrontation on the direction they want the school to take. Guta preaches Socialist Zionism, which the rabbi sees as incompatible with the teachings of the Torah. It's up to Esther to reestablish order in the ranks. Jacob, to simplify matters, would rather kick out Zionism and the Torah since he loathes them both. Now he swears only by a radical-leaning Yiddishism. Indeed, the Lipshitzes are militant Bundists, especially Helena who has converted a rather "Polonized" Jacob. It's thanks to Helena that he's relearned our language. It's thanks to Esther that he'll relearn the language of love; she's certain that these two don't love each other, at least not anymore. Such a school was established at the start of last summer. When it was discovered, the teachers were shot and the students sent God-knows-where. That's what Esther tried to tell Hannah: the enterprise is not without danger. Hannah almost smiled, yes, smiled, and I answered her smile. "We don't have any choice." Esther would have liked to take her in her arms at that moment and waltz her around humming Chopin. But she didn't dare. Such reactions toward people are very rare in her. When, a few years ago, she was a little in love with Zofia who lived upstairs, she began to read the Gospels and books on the life of Jesus. Those days, when she went out, she wanted to kiss and hug passers-by to tell them that she loved them. You're on the right path, Zofia told her. But by chance those books fell into Momma's hands, and she screamed bloody murder and told Adek. Papa immediately recognized Zofia's influence. He decided the better course of wisdom was to minimize the incident so as not to stir up his daughter's rebellious disposition and have a greater scandal on his hands. His systematic opposition would push her, by pure spirit of contradiction, into converting, God preserve us, to Christianity. And the "crisis" passed. The Litvaks did not have to go into mourning, cover their heads with ashes. A few years earlier, when Esther was still a child, she had found, in a bookstore on Jerozolimska Boulevard, a print of the Virgin of Jasna Gora at Czestochowa. She had thought her so beautiful that she bought the print. When she got home, she showed it proudly to her mother who had a fit and demanded that Esther return it to the bookstore.

How Esther had hated her mother then! "What, her beautiful! Oy, are you completely *mishuge!*"

Szymon's arms seem very scrawny. Besides, we're all losing weight. Freydla tried to grow some vegetables in wooden boxes on the balcony. Last night, as we were getting ready to eat them we noticed they still weren't ripe. Yanek was so sad. I caught Momma hiding provisions inside the *Tennis Player*, perhaps jewelry. No one would think of lifting a sculpture this heavy.

O

Decree of the *Judenrat*: All men between the ages of eighteen and thirty-five must be ready to leave for labor camps. They can be called at any moment. A German high up in rank has proclaimed, "If Germany wins the war, the Jewish question will be solved in three months; if it loses the war, in one hour." What's so hard to admit is that he's speaking the truth. And the truth is that we're in the midst of two wars, the war the Germans wage against the nations and the war they wage against the Jews. These are two separate wars, and the outcome of the former has no effect on the latter. This is what Jews don't understand. As for the other nations, they're rather busy right now. The Germans are bombing their cities, and they understand that there's a war going on. The Jews are being decimated, but they wonder, "perhaps if . . . , do you think that . . . , sometimes it . . . , how to know where. . . ." They *speculate*. Everyone has his own agenda—Bundists, Communists, Zionists of the left, of the right, of the center. The religious Jews await the coming of the Messiah. He's the one, they say, who will answer their questions. But will we still be here to receive him? Or, granted, he'll give us an answer, but the question will have disappeared. Along with us who ask it. Perhaps the war will end in a few months from now. That's the rumor among pious Jews. Meanwhile, the men must avoid the labor camps. They can "buy themselves back" for a sum averaging between ten and twenty-five zlotys, which goes into the *Judenrat's* coffers. Since rumor has it that the Germans take only bachelors, Szymon has asked me to marry him. This kind of proposal, that is, marriage for material reasons, seemed to me suddenly acceptable. All the same, I ran it by Freydla and she advised me to wait. Why? "Let's wait and see how things turn out," was all I could get from her.

The Hasidim await the end of the war as they await the Messiah. That is, they calculate the date of A. H.'s defeat by counting the different verses of the Torah and adding the numerical value of their letters. Huberband, our Orthodox rabbi, rejects such calculation as not "kosher."

Last night, during our committee meeting, talk turned to Adam Czerniakow, the president of the Jewish Council. The majority of self-righteous Jews feel that this "martyr" is sacrificing himself for all our sakes. Here, we think otherwise: this character is in fact an ally of the Germans.

O

Why shouldn't I marry Szymon? He's the first man I got to know. He's the first man who will know me.

O

We're becoming increasingly concerned about the German plan to build a ghetto. More and more Jews are being expelled from the neighborhoods located outside of the "epidemic zone." Since they're given very short notice that they must move, in most cases they have to leave all their possessions behind. Talk centers on the probable perimeters of the ghetto. The ghetto will likely stretch at least between Zlota and Pawia streets, perhaps even further north, toward Stawki and Bonifraterska. The Jews of Zlota Street hope that they'll be included in the ghetto so as not to have to move, losing their apartments and probably their furniture. But the Poles of Zlota outnumber the Jews and want that street for themselves. We're being pushed into wishing that the ghetto becomes a reality, and as soon as possible. Because then we'll be left alone: we won't have to deal with the Germans anymore. We're rationalizing as we've done before, as we have always done. We have always known massacres—that's nothing new, is it? And yet, we're still here, aren't we? And besides, in the ghetto we were safe. The gates were locked at night and the *goyim* could do us no harm. So what would be so terrible about a ghetto here, in Warsaw?

They don't know what to wish for anymore, what to hope for, what to think. They don't know anything anymore. Soon they'll be going around in circles like wild beasts in their cages. They'll *become* wild beasts, and the *goyim*, outside the cage, won't be shy about shooting inside.

Unfortunately, the problem with Zlota Street is that many Jews bought apartments there recently.

O

This morning, a German soldier slapped Esther very hard while she was going to Szymon's house on Krochmalna Street. She fell on the pavement. The soldier yelled at her for not having yielded the sidewalk to him. She simply hadn't seen him. What was she dreaming about? She arrived in tears at Szymon's house, her whole body shaking, her teeth chattering as she cried: she couldn't stop crying. She doesn't remember ever having been in such a state. Szymon took her in his arms, and asked questions. But she couldn't talk. Then he tried to kiss her on the mouth. Esther pushed him away, ready to slap him, ready, yes, to slap him as the German had slapped her. Finally, calming down, she apologized. I don't know what came over me. She sat on his lap. Szymon stroked her hair as Daddy used to do. Then, lifting me off his lap, he went to fetch his large cap lying on a shelf and placed it on my head, and looked at me for a long time. Then Szymon took Esther by the hand, led her to the free-standing mirror, and stared at her reflection. They stood there for a long time, he looking with admiration at her reflection, and Esther seeing herself through Szymon's eyes. I think that we were happy. I shouldn't think about Jacob anymore. Indeed, it had been Jacob I was thinking of on the way to Szymon's house. I mustn't think about him anymore: I could lose everything.

O

The eve of Rosh Hashanah. They say that from now on Jewish men will have to wear a cap and Jewish women a scarf. I'll wear a cap, Szymon's cap. Tonight, on the eve of the New Year, there'll be fourteen of us for dinner. The rabbi tried to talk us into going to *shul*, but without success. Freydla made fish and soup. Rabbi Huberband will recite the prayers. Adek predicts that this might be the last time we'll be able to celebrate Rosh Hashanah in this way. How ridiculous to wish each other *shana tova* or, in Yiddish, a *gut yor*, a good year!

Szymon told me about this incident. People were fighting on one of the streetcars. An old couple was arguing in Polish. "If you want to yell at each other," someone screamed, "at least do it in Yiddish. This is a Jewish streetcar here, a streetcar with the *mogen Dovid*, with the star." "Not at all! You should talk in Hebrew. Hebrew is our language," screamed someone else. And a third person, a young, well-dressed man said, "We have the perfect right to speak Polish. Even a Jew has the right to speak Polish." "And why not German while you're at it?" cried another. "Why not German indeed?" said someone else. "I studied liberal arts in Germany. German is the most beautiful language, the most rigorous, the most logical, the most subtle, the most. . . ." But he was prevented from finishing his sentence. All the other passengers fell on him, screaming, "In Yiddish, in Yiddish. Talk in Yiddish." And during a brief lull in the storm, someone yelled, "A Jew who doesn't speak Yiddish is no longer a Jew. In his heart he is already a *goy*." The old couple had stopped arguing and left the streetcar without anyone noticing. But the funniest thing about this scene, Szymon concluded, was that they all expressed themselves absolutely fluently in the languages they were defending—German, Polish, Yiddish, or Hebrew.

Our enemies are right: we are cosmopolitan and stateless.

A scene like that would obviously have been impossible before the war. First of all, there were no such things as Jewish streetcars. Now that Jews have been brought together by the force of circumstances—circumstances being the Germans—they no longer stand on ceremony. For example, our streetcars are much dirtier than the goyish streetcars. Why? Because we feel at home now. We joke as much as we want. Therefore Saxony Platz has been rebaptized Adolf Hitler Platz, and when the streetcar stops there and the conductor announces in a sinister voice, *Adolf Hitler Platz!*, everybody answers, as in *shul*, *Amen!* In Yiddish "Adolf Hitler Platz" means "Adolf Hitler drop dead."

○

The ghetto is official, the loudspeakers announced. Jews have until the end of the month to settle in and Poles to clear out. There's more moving in and out than ever. Apartments are exchanged any which way. Rumors are that the *Judenrat* will create a corps of a thousand Jewish policemen to be in charge of directing traffic. Papa is in constant and mysterious negotiations with a Jew who knows another Jew who knows the "financial advisor" of the German who has total control over Jewish businesses located in the Aryan Zone. The (provisional) result of all these dealings—a million zlotys, an amount still to be agreed on, but which would include payoffs to all the middlemen. Esther knows that Adek won't hesitate to pay.

The educator Janusz Korczak has just been arrested for not wearing his Jewish badge. I always wondered if he had converted or simply changed his name. Or if he is as great a writer as some people claim he is. But no one escapes the Germans. His kindergarten was destroyed.

On our side, the greatest anxiety now is learning that your street is excluded from the ghetto. Especially if, after much trouble, you've just moved in. Then you have to move out again. Some people have moved half a dozen times. I couldn't stand that. Yet, we've moved often since I was born.

The Polish police are going to leave the ghetto. People stock up with whatever they can get their hands on. Momma doesn't lag behind. She fusses like a real *yidishe mame*, helping those in need, those hit by typhus. The wall is rising rapidly. In the streets people rush about as if on the eve of a holiday. In order to avoid trouble, Chaim and Guta have moved in with the Litvaks, leaving their own place to some refugees. All they had to bring down was their bedding. Freydla doesn't ask anything of me, ever. Nathan, Adek's brother, has left for the Soviet Zone. In a letter transmitted to us, he asks us to join him. Freydla says we can still wait. Tszupek, our porter, had to leave: Poles can no longer work for Jews (the opposite doesn't hold true). He insisted on saying his goodbyes to Esther, complimenting her on the way she takes care of Yanek and of the clandestine school. Was he being ironic? I hope he'll hold his tongue.

Adek thinks his shop is lost once and for all. The ghetto is locked. This morning, he came down very early, checking a dozen times to make sure he was carrying the pass his "provisional administrator" consented to sell him. His name is Handschuh, *"glove,"* or, literally, "hand-shoe." An example of the elegance of the German language.

Adek took the same path he always takes, past Karmel-icka and Franciszkanska, in the direction of Bonifrater-ska Street. And there, in the middle of Bonifraterska, appeared a barricade of barbed wires. German soldiers prevented people from passing through. So Adek waved Herr Hand-Shoe's letter under the nose of a soldier who was content to simply shake his head no—he was so polite. Pushed back by the surging crowd that had formed, a fat resigned-looking lady walked by in front of Adek and, without speaking to him in particular, said in Yiddish that no one could pass anymore, that was it, they were all locked in. Adek came back home and went to bed. Freydla makes him some tea. Esther doesn't dare try to console him.

O

It's *Shabbes* today. Esther is writing *in* the ghetto. Adek hasn't gotten up. One of his *goy* friends, perhaps a former customer, brought us some bread. Adek didn't bother getting up to see him. He stayed in the dark, curtains drawn.

Something terrible happened to Szymon, worse than the slap I got. Having gone to look for food in the Polish Quarter, he was spotted by some Germans. They grabbed him, told him to lie down on his stomach in the mud, and four of them trampled him. Esther is afraid. She wants to be with Szymon all the time. She admits to herself that she needs him.

Yiddish has become fashionable. Polonized artists now sing in this language. The fashion is also given to wearing boots like the Germans. The worm is fascinated by the star. It's very cold. Minus fifteen degrees and hardly anything to use for heat.

Jacob Lipshitz is going to join the Jewish police. As an intellectual, what else can he do? The Jewish Council approved his application. They gave him a cap, a belt, a white stick, and a badge. His dark blue cap has a star of David on the visor. He wears his badge on his chest. Esther thinks he looks splendid. He'll assume his duties on December 20th, at first being assigned traffic control at the corner of Dzielna and Karmelicka. After all, Esther told Szymon (not believing a word of it), to join the Jewish police is like resisting the Germans. Tragic, major error, says Szymon: the Jewish police is and always will be only an efficient tool of the Germans. "I know the Jews," he said with a wise look. They're willing to compromise a little and, step by step, the limits of the morally tolerable are pushed back further and further until a person is reduced to openly collaborating and then becomes an accomplice. "And you, you're always ready to stick up for him. You're totally blind as far as that character is concerned. Is it because he's handsome that you're so ready to excuse him? Because he loves literature and music? So do the Germans!"

The converts are preparing their Christmas tree. Some of them earn a living by selling herring provided by some charitable organization. This reminds Esther of the herrings of Ptachia Street that Adek told her so often about. On the street where he went to school there was a courtyard filled with barrels of herring, so that every night when he went home his clothes reeked of the persistent odor. "It's not my fault," he would tell Raisl, his mother, "it's the herring of Ptachia Street!" And he would always burst out laughing when he told this story. As for the converts, with or without their Christmas trees, the fact that they're selling herring to Jews, in a ghetto, speaks volumes about their situation. Who besides Jews could sell herring to Jews! In a ghetto!

Jacob is a daily witness to German extortion. The scene is always identical. A truck drives at full speed into the Jewish crowd. It stops, the Germans alight, and all the Jews scatter, panic-stricken. Rare is the person who can keep calm, stay put, remove his hat. The others are caught, beaten savagely when they're not trampled like rugs. A few children die from hard blows to the head.

Here, everyone scribbles in his journal, everyone thinks he's a writer. As well they should. To be a writer means nothing anymore. To become one means even less. Here, there is no "becoming" that lasts. Nothing lasts anymore except a small, fragile breath of life, very tenuous. This breath of life is our hope that the British will come, but it's a fragile breath, because more and more we think that they'll cry victory over our coffins.

O

The Zionists, especially those from *Hashomer Hatzair*, are waging an intense propaganda campaign for people to join them, to prepare for the future in Palestine. Szymon has adopted their motto: "Survival is not enough." Shady lawyers are signing deeds to land in the Galilee. Everything is for sale in the ghetto. Even death becomes a source of profit. You can grant yourself a luxurious burial complete with undertakers in uniform. A certain Pinkert, nicknamed the King of the Dead, is opening branch after branch of his funeral-parlor business. This is his busy season—a hundred deaths per week.

Last night Jacob came home very upset. He knocked at the door wanting to talk to someone. In spite of myself I smiled on hearing his words. He didn't smile. Here's what happened: he was directing traffic at the corner of Zelazna and Grzybowska. Jews in rags wsere standing there, waiting for the opportunity to sneak into the Aryan sector. Jacob was watching them out of the corner of his eye, slightly anxious and somewhat amused by a vendor, at the other side of the crossroad, who was yelling, "If you need a rag, buy a brand new one!" Suddenly a German policeman appeared and ordered Jacob to quickly disperse the group of Jews. Jacob moved toward them and gave the order to move. They ignored him and didn't budge. He yelled at them, "you used to respect Polish policemen before, why don't you obey a Jewish policeman now?" But no one paid him any attention; it was as if he were invisible. The German policeman waited a few more minutes, then, without a word of warning, shot into the crowd. Three Jews were killed.

Why did Jacob insist on telling this to Esther and not to Helena?

O

Purim. This will be the greatest Purim of all times. The Jews have the perfect Haman—A. H.

Adek gave Esther some money to buy Yiddish books. They're so cheap now. She and Hannah Krawetz bought them by the basket. They sort them and classify them. They open some at random and start reading. Esther's favorite author is Peretz. She reads passages aloud to her friend, who admires her ability to read Yiddish so well. Hannah tries but stumbles on the Hebrew expressions; her real culture is Polish.

Hannah is a real *cordon bleu*. She has delicious Jewish recipes from her grandmother. Recently, she cooked us a traditional *Shabbes* dish, a *chulent*. Freydla got her all the necessary ingredients, God knows how: potatoes, beans, etc. . . . Before the war, Hannah was engaged to an eternal student of medicine, Misha Peltzman, who today is a psychiatrist, a happy-go-lucky fellow who loved to laugh and tell dirty jokes. And devour Hannah's cooking. Like Nathan Litvak he went over to the Soviet Zone, and he writes Hannah to come join him. But she doesn't want to leave her little pupils on Okopowa Street. Esther tells her she's wrong.

More than anything else, Hannah loves French literature, especially Victor Hugo's poetry, which she reads
in French and in Polish. We found some of his poems
translated into Yiddish in one of the boxes. Esther memo-
rized the poem *Contemplations*, which tells of the taking
of Jericho by Joshua. Hannah and Esther recite it together, Hannah in French, Esther in Yiddish. Again
and again:

*À la septième fois les murailles tombèrent**
Baym zibetn arumgeyn iz di moyer ayngefaln

Who will circle the ghetto seven times for us and blow
the *shofar* until the wall comes toppling down? The British? The Russians? Or the Angel of Death?

O

Szymon is becoming more and more adamant about
Esther marrying him. She finds him sweet, intelligent,
rather subtle, yes, subtle for a scientist. But she's not
madly in love with him. And furthermore, there is the
war, the wall, all these beggars, people dying every day
of hunger, of cold, of typhus, of a German bullet caught
trying to sneak into the Aryan sector, all that. Were she
to give in to his wishes, Esther would have the terrible
feeling that her hand was being forced, that something
was deciding for her. And then, another thing, which she
tells no one because it seems so incongruous and childish,
but she thinks that if she married Szymon, or anyone
else for that matter, her writing would slip through her

*The seventh time, the walls came toppling down.

41

fingers. It's as if the book that she'll write someday is already formed, and waiting for her at the end of a path she follows blindly but intuitively. If she should take another path, she'll miss this book. That's what Esther thinks. A childish thought, granted, but she wants to be a child, keep on being a little girl. If, through some misfortune, she were to have to give it up, let's say in order to be happy, then life would have no meaning. Might as well die. Might as well die than be like everybody else. Mediocre, like everybody else.

Esther accepts the fact that Szymon is in love with her. She lets him love her. She even asks for that kind of love. After all, it's no small matter to inspire love in someone. And what if it were only desire? So what? It's just as beautiful to inspire desire. And when Szymon becomes too adamant, she answers, "after the war." Because there are two possibilities. Either he's really in love with her, but what he calls "love" is only a result of the desire he feels for her, in which case, once satisfied, his desire will disappear. Or, he feels only desire for her, and eventually his desire will fade away. And besides, everyone knows what marriage is like. Which is why she says "after the war." To which Szymon replies, "there'll be no after the war for us." To which I then reply, "In that case, it doesn't matter." Szymon has no answer to that. We both keep quiet then. We hold hands. . . . "Meanwhile, I'll keep on making love to *Hashomer Hatzair*." This comment, which he made yesterday, brought tears to Esther's eyes—tears of laughter. And you should have seen what he looked like then, staring at the floor, half dazed, half tragic.

Besides, what does "happiness" mean? Let others try to be happy, and if they succeed, so much the better for them.

O

First night of Passover. Will the prophet Elijah be allowed on the streets after nine o'clock at night? He could always show his identity card if the Germans don't shoot him first. But would that make an impression?

Guta was in charge of inviting our friends. Yanek, the youngest among us, will ask the traditional questions, "Why is this night different from all other nights?" I suppose that Reb Huberband and Adek will take turns reading the Haggadah and translating into Polish. Jacob asked Guta to invite his cousin, someone named Wladek, which Guta refused vehemently; from what she's heard, this Wladek is involved in shady deals. She suspects that he has connections with the Gestapo. A Jewish policeman, okay, but I draw the line at a Jewish collaborator. Jacob nodded and didn't try to argue. Szymon, who was present during this conversation, took the opportunity to denigrate Jacob again: isn't he in his way a collaborator? When the Germans ask for fifteen hundred men for their labor camps, if indeed they really are labor camps, and only fifty volunteer, who goes man-hunting if not the Jewish police? That he doesn't talk about, your Jacob, but everybody knows it, everybody sees it. Well, why don't you say that to his face? You can't, no, you're too cowardly to do it, Szymon. Deep down, he's afraid to confront Jacob. Esther doesn't want it either. It would be a catastrophe for everyone. Especially for her.

Adek pays a hundred zlotys every month so that Mathiek won't be called. The rich will probably be able to manage. (Some of the rich have become the poorest of the poor and vice versa.) The raids strike indiscriminately; luck is democratic. But the rich pay either the police or the doctors who exempt them. Thus the old order is restored: when a poor man is picked up, there's no way for him to escape deportation. That's what happens to those walking dead, mostly refugees, who already are dying of hunger.

○

Jacob hinted to Martha that he plans to resign from the Jewish police. He's witnessed enough horror. He's had his fill. Esther suspects that by "horrors witnessed" he means "horrors committed." There's no way she can ask Szymon for his opinion. Besides, she already knows what he thinks. But the fact that Jacob is resigning from the police gives her a strong argument against Szymon. But what vain and ridiculous game is she playing? Why should Szymon like Jacob? What good would it do her?

Thanks to the influence of Jacob's cousin, this famous Wladek, Martha Lipshitz will probably have a job playing the piano in a cabaret, a sort of café-restaurant on Leszno Street. Martha is very pretty. Esther can't deny it. And on top of it, she looks Aryan, like her mother. The question is what did she have to *pay* for this job? And to whom?

Mathiek, Martha Lipshitz, and Reb Huberband are growing vegetables on a free plot next to the grave of Reb Huberband's wife in the Jewish cemetery. But Mathiek has heard rumors that soon the cemetery will be placed outside the ghetto borders.

Esther overheard Freydla and Adek arguing. Her father gave Reb Nuss, a Bundist and one of his acquaintances, as an example. Nuss had become a citizen of Uruguay and so was able to get out through the Aryan sector. Freydla spoke of escape, of cowardice. Then they talked about Nathan who had gone over to the Soviet

Zone. He had the right idea, Adek yelled, he did the right thing. And how do you know that he did the right thing? How do you know that there he eats more than we do, Momma retorted. Then, Adek mentioned Wladek, Jacob's cousin. What did she think of him? Did she think he was also wrong? Esther understood then the kind of activities Wladek was involved in. He belongs to a group that "fights against speculators," an official organization connected to the Germans, whose noble task it is to catch smugglers and make them pay. Don't you dare hang out with such people, Freydla screamed. It's one thing trying to protect yourself, to earn zlotys, but not by bloodying your hands! Adek went back to bed.

O

Esther has reason to believe that her brother is in love with Martha Lipshitz. Apparently an unrequited love. He's in bed with a bad flu. In this he's really very much like his father: if things don't go his way he's anxious, and right away, he's "sick." Esther nurses Mathiek. That consists mostly in listening as he confides in her, not holding back. Martha doesn't want to "go with him." The other day, she even cried when he became unbearably insistent. Martha claims that a great career awaits her— well, well. And a Litvak is perhaps not good enough for her then? As he left, Mathiek called her *kurva*, whore. But he didn't even have time to regret it because she slapped him. He tried to apologize but Martha ran away, sobbing loudly on the stairs. Then Mathiek began to scream insults at her again, reminding her of the activities of her cousin Wladek who's now a sort of go-between or god-knows-what middleman between the Gestapo and that virtuous band fighting the "smugglers." Martha put

45

her hands over her ears, refusing to hear any more, and ran up the stairs. So now Mathiek has the flu. Esther suggested that he go see the Lipshitzes and apologize to Martha.

O

Is the agenda of the day really to prepare us to go to Palestine? Are the Zionists forgetting that we're locked up in a ghetto? Guta lost her temper at the way the Lipshitzes view the problem, like a caricature. The agenda of the day, she said, is well and good to fight the Germans. And what are the rest of us doing if not resisting when we run off tracts in basements, listen to clandestine radios, publish our newspapers, come what may? But our enemies are less the Germans and the Ukrainians than some of our own corrupt people, Gestapo agents drawing a shameless profit from our suffering. Jacob is well acquainted with people like that; he knows what I mean. Jews asking thirty zlotys from other Jews threatened by deportation—yes, yes, he knew all about that, he played along. And those people organizing cultural evenings, and running charity works that are simply fronts for their real pursuits, the scoundrels—he knows about that too, he sure does.

Szymon says that *Hashomer* is going to entrust Guta with a mission outside the ghetto.

O

The streets are littered with naked corpses covered over with newspapers. At dawn, Pinkert carts collect them for burial in common graves in the cemeteries where tourists, in and out of uniform, stroll about admiring the hundreds of corpses waiting to be interred. The Germans take pictures.

Last night, Adek began to talk about leaving the ghetto, about crossing over to the Aryan side. "Do I look Jewish?" he keeps asking his annoyed wife. He could memorize some goyish prayers, wouldn't that be a good idea? His question was met with a loaded silence. Wladek, Lipshitz's cousin whom he had met, told him of a doctor who "rectified" circumcisions. . . . We were appalled. "Okay. Let's drop it . . . But I still have many Polish friends there . . ." You could have cried. Because of his stupidity. Now Esther hates her father. "Many Polish friends." How can he still think that way knowing what we know?

O

Mathiek dreams only of marrying Martha Lipshitz. She wouldn't say no. Her parents don't know anything about it. But Reb Huberband does. And Guta. And Esther.

Guta is gone. Why her and not Esther, especially since Guta is married? Perhaps Szymon wanted to spare Esther, thinking the undertaking too dangerous. But why doesn't he mind his own business? What rights does he have over me? I'll never marry him, never, he can wait forever.

O

Adek left them. Did they have tears in their eyes? Yes, they did. He had to get beyond the gates at the end of Leszno Street, mingle with a team of workers from Karolkowa, which runs perpendicular to the cemetery and is outside the ghetto, and bribe the team boss.

47

Esther bragged to Yanek about her father's resourcefulness!

Guta's leaving affects her at least as much. She imagines all the dangers she's facing, fears for her, admires her. She should be away about twenty days. She doesn't know exactly what her mission is.

Before leaving, Adek gave two thousand zlotys to Dr. Kaufman, their doctor before the war, to vaccinate them against typhus. They say that this winter one out of five Jews will die of typhus. The Pinkert brothers are making a fortune from the corpses. Adek must have remembered all of a sudden that he was *paterfamilias*. The paternal instinct is stronger than anything else, isn't it?

The Germans will lose the war. It seems that even the *Volksdeutsche* believe it. Meanwhile we are all dying, one after the other.

O

Esther spent last night on Muranowska Street, at the home of some friends of Szymon. Children begging and screaming way past the curfew, and she threw them some bread. Around midnight, one child was still screaming, sitting on the sidewalk beneath the window. Esther opened the shutters and threw down another piece of bread. Then she saw that the child was lying down, motionless, his hand stretched out. In the morning he was dead, still in the same position, his hand stretched out. Esther climbed over the little corpse; it was covered by a newspaper held in place by a brick. The child's open palm stuck out from under the newspaper.

Entire families go begging together. Whole families are dying of hunger together, the same night. Or one of them doesn't quite die immediately but lingers several days, waiting for death as rats gnaw at the other corpses. The *Judenrat* and the Jewish police maintain order. Order above all else. No pushing and shoving, there'll be enough death to go around.

Guta came back from Vilna with overwhelming evidence of systematic massacres in Bialystok, even in Vilna. This news was transmitted to the *Judenrat*. The main thing is not to panic everyone, they said. Thus, mum's the word, *shhh*. *Shhh* on the death of Jews. And we're protesting the silence of nations, the silence of God, the silence of I don't know what! While our own representatives. . . . It's true that they don't represent us: they do the Germans' handiwork.

○

Rosh Hashanah. I miss Daddy so much it hurts. I never would have thought it. There's no news from him. It would be impossible for him to write. He warned us. Freydla remains impassive. She feels that she's getting sick. She can't get rid of her lice; they keep multiplying.

○

Freydla is dead. We found her in the morning. Her face was distorted in pain. Rabbi Huberband took care of everything. Mathiek recited the *Kaddish*.

○

Esther placed her brother in Dr. Korczak's children's home. She visits him every day. Hannah Krawetz told her about it, praising its merits and those of Doctor Korczak with his genuine love of children. At first Dr. Korczak was very reluctant to take Yanek: his home is already very crowded. It's a home for real orphans, children without parents or relatives, et cetera. . . . Resorting to her father's methods, Esther offered to make a significant contribution to the home: it worked.

They say that the Jews of Warsaw will be transferred to the East. Or all Jews under the General Government. Or that they'll be transferred to a special "Jewish homeland." There are so many rumors; impossible to sort out the true from the false.

According to Reb Huberband, the war will end this year: the numerical value of the new Jewish year, 5702, is equal to that of the word *shabbat*. This is truly a bad sign, that he's starting to count on this sort of thing.

Every year the Germans demonstrate their solicitude. For Rosh Hashanah of the year 5700 it was the bombings. For 5701, the creation of the ghetto. 5702, our space is further reduced: they're talking of abolishing the smaller ghetto, Sienna Street in particular. What will 5703 bring? Will we still be celebrating Rosh Hashanah then?

O

Esther had a dream that night. She was giving birth to a child. Szymon was at her side, happy, serene. Then he asked whether it was a boy or a girl. She didn't know. Szymon began to feel for the baby in the dark, as if it were Esther, but he couldn't find its sex. Then he remarked that the baby wasn't crying. No, said Esther, it didn't cry, no one heard it. Szymon then shook the baby a little bit as if it were a rag doll. The baby remained inert. It was dead. Szymon burst into tears. Esther was shocked but she showed no emotion. She knew that the baby was dead but she said nothing. Was she indifferent or fighting back her pain? She doesn't know. What she does know, however, is that she'll never have children, never. And also that she'll never be a writer. She knows. She'll die first. Or rather, it's the other way around: she'll die because she has no child in her womb and no book from her hand.

O

The first snow fell. The corpses of seventeen people dead from the cold.

O

Frozen corpses of children in the street. Hundreds of Jews, children and grown-ups, walk barefoot in the snow.

O

What optimism on the part of the French poet Victor Hugo to think that the sound of Joshua's *shofar* alone could shatter the walls of Jericho! Rest assured, A. H. is altogether different from Napoleon III, as are the walls of Jericho from our wall. Who will sound the *shofar* that topples the ghetto walls to free us—the Russians, the English? Is there a Victor Hugo pleading for us somewhere in the world? Every night I hear the heart-rending cries of children dying of hunger on the corner of Nowolipie and Karmelicka. Who will echo these cries?

Helena Lipshitz has weakened a lot, and grows thinner by the day. Esther feels guilty, which is stupid. Last night they were all together at the Lipshitzes'. Everyone had brought something to make a fire. Martha sat down at the piano and played to gratify her father's pride and my brother's affection. Helena sat by herself, as though absent, the dark circles like blackish stains around her eyes, more and more pronounced. When Martha had tired of playing, they recited poetry. Esther again recited Victor Hugo's poem, first in French thanks to Hannah's efforts to teach her, then in Yiddish (she refused to do it in Polish). Why does this poem obsess her so? Why, as soon as she first read it, did she memorize it? Why does she recite it to herself sometimes at night when she can't sleep, when she thinks of the children moaning in the street? And also of Adek and Freydla? And of Yanek, abandoned, yes, abandoned. No, not abandoned, since she visits him every day, sees that he eats his fill, at least so he doesn't lose weight. But abandoned all the same.

Esther spoke to Szymon about the poem and her "obsession." He, of course, thinks there's something sexual hiding in it. No matter how hard she looks, she doesn't see anything sexual in the poem. Could he be more specific? But he can't be. Perhaps the granite tower, so high and hard, is a sort of symbol. But of what? Szymon had kept several of Doctor Freud's books; he'll give them to her. But that's his stock answer because each time he "forgets."

Martha is not as great a virtuoso as Esther suspected. Or as she dreaded. Her playing is even rather belabored, strained, brusque. And she really gets on her nerves. Her frivolous side, so indifferent to what's happening. In truth, she lacks personality, which perhaps is not unrelated to her Polish looks. Her beauty, in other words. Girls who know they are beautiful think they're exempt from being intelligent. They think they can do whatever they want. They seduce only by appearances. To think that I have so little influence on Mathiek. I hadn't even realized.

○

Books are being sold on Leszno Street by the basketful, by weight. Books in English are especially prized because people dream of emigrating to America after the war. Esther would prefer Paris, Szymon too. Esther would like her children to speak the language of Victor Hugo. What children? Oh yes, those she'll have in another life, in her next reincarnation . . .

1812. That's the date that you can see scribbled on every poster in the ghetto. It refers to Napoleon's having sunk down in this mire . . .

○

Yesterday morning Wladek, always well informed, warned Jacob that something was afoot for the evening or that night. Our plan was to hide in the cellar after we'd gathered enough food and water. Then it was agreed that only the women would go down. Then Guta decided she'd stay with the men, and Martha and my brother wanted to go out. Jacob lost his temper and forbade it. Martha provoked him. Wasn't she free to go for a walk if she wanted? She managed to slip out like a fish escaping the net. Desperate, Jacob took his head in his hands. Helena didn't intervene. These days she's overcome with grief and just waits for death.

Esther's feeling was that they wanted to go out to make love, and she took their side against Jacob. Had Szymon been there, she would have given herself to him; she felt like it. Did this sudden desire have any connection with the looming night of terror? Finally Helena, Guta, and Hannah went down to the cellar, followed by Reb Huberband. Did he consider himself a woman or what? Esther refused. Szymon wasn't there and she wanted—like him, at the same time as him, linked to him in spirit—to run the same risks. Was he hiding with his mother in his own building or did he join his friends in *Hashomer*?

Jacob paced circles around the living room lit only by the faint light of a candle. He was mad at himself for having let his daughter go out. It really isn't fun for young lovers to live with ten other people, without ever having a single moment alone, tête-à-tête. Jacob didn't respond to Esther's comment. He kept pacing the room. Esther stared at the frail light. Mathiek and Martha were risking death, deportation. Even if she, Esther, was so happy that they're in love, so pleased at their embracing somewhere in an unconsecrated and sordid spot in the ghetto, she couldn't deny that they might fall into the hands of the Germans. He stared at her. Had she just given out a cry? Suddenly, deep down, she felt a painful feeling of envy. They had just made love when the Germans appeared. . . . Who, they? Martha and her brother, or she and Jacob? Was she willing to see the Germans break down the door of the apartment so that Jacob could take her in his arms and caress her and. . . ? He would probably spend the whole evening pacing the floor of that room, his hand stroking the beard sprouting on his cheek, so handsome. Esther went up to bed without even a goodnight. Esther didn't exist for him and he didn't exist for her, that's all.

She couldn't sleep. It must have been one in the morning when she heard a quick and heavy step climbing the stairs, then a soft knock on the door. It must be Mathiek coming home to bed. She went to open the door: it was

Szymon, very upset, out of breath. His name was on the list, the list that the Jewish police pass to the Germans with the names of all sorts of militants. The Jewish police lead the Germans to the addresses given them by informers. And his mother? He thought that she was safe.

In a hurried and hoarse voice (more upset, thought Esther, at being alone with her in her room than by events), he related in detail the complicated itinerary he had followed to come from Krochmalna Street to Nowolipie, the porches under which he'd hidden, the courtyards he'd crossed, tripping over corpses, at least he thought they were corpses because it was too dark to tell.

To shut him up, Esther put her hand on his mouth, to stop hearing those horrors, to calm him. Her thoughts strayed, went back to those two young idiots and their night of love. She was older, wasn't she? So then, why them before her, was that fair?

Let Szymon come to bed. Let him undress. She tried to meet his eyes but he wasn't looking at her, too preoccupied. Look, he undresses without thinking, as though we were married, and he slips under the covers conjugally . . .

Explosions in the street, some close by, others further away.

Wasn't it ridiculous, to be a virgin at twenty? His Polish girlfriends . . .

○

The Germans are filming the ghetto, focusing on the *Judenrat* on Grzybowska Street and the Jewish prison on Gesia where half the detainees are children who tried to crawl through gaps in the wall. Our depravities, our wickedness will live on forever thanks to some skillful movie making. With that in mind, the Germans gathered a crowd of Jews on Smocza Street and ordered Jewish policemen to disperse them brutally. Which the latter did with their usual submissiveness. German soldiers were filmed rescuing a Jewish child who had sneaked through a breach in the wall and who was being threatened by a Jewish or Polish policeman. The German, good soldier that he is, tells them not to beat children. German tourists have just been forbidden to visit our cemetery. It seems that piles of corpses in a hut near the Rebbe of Radzymin's mausoleum create a bad impression, and sometimes even elicit some objections on their part.

They are shooting more and more people in the streets. According to our Jews, it's because of the Communists, the Zionists, the Bundists and their criminal propaganda. Always harping on the same string. Meanwhile, Guta practices saying "Holy Mother of Czestochowa!" and "By the wounds of Christ." It reminds me of my little Zofia who used to say that all the time. What became of her in the Aryan sector?

Once again, Guta is being sent out of the ghetto. She wears a crucifix. When she crosses the wall, she'll exchange her cap for a scarf. She asked me yesterday if, as people tell her, she really has *an arishn punim*, an Aryan look, which sounds a lot like *a narishn punim*, which means a stupid look. In truth, she has neither an Aryan nor a stupid look. It's Martha who's best suited for this kind of mission. *Holy Mother of Czestochowa! By the wounds of Christ!* I'm crazy about these idolatrous magic formulas.

O

Yesterday Chaim witnessed a horrible scene at the corner of Twarda and Sliska streets. The Germans had set a long table with bottles of wine and piles of food. Then a truck arrived and a dozen young Hasidim were brought down. They lined them up along the table while other Germans collected all the starving children they could find nearby on Prosta Street and massed them on the sidewalk: children in rags, bare-footed, bellies swollen by hunger. Then as the cameras rolled, the Germans ordered the Hasidim to gorge themselves on the food and wine, then dance and sing. And the pitiful little beggars stared at them, imploring—that was the whole point of the filming—as the Hasidim had to forcefully push them back. Then, when this masterpiece was filmed, they put away their movie cameras, and another truck drove up full of soldiers—those with skull-and-crossbones looks—and they machine-gunned the children and Hasidim together, before the eyes of a terrorized crowd.

O

Some people have listened to BBC broadcasts giving information on our fate in the ghettos and especially in various camps, Chelmno, Belzec. Speculation has it that seven hundred thousand Jews have been killed up to now. Why is the whole world silent? Why does the Polish government in exile minimize what is happening to us? Why pass it over in silence? For what purpose? For the purpose, says Szymon, of establishing that the Polish people are the primary victims of the Germans, and not the Jews. Two martyred peoples are one too many. Some say that it's not the first persecution we've known and it won't be the last. There were the Crusades, the Spanish Inquisition, the Ukrainian massacres, the czarist pogroms, yet the Jewish people still live. They say that we must not provoke the Germans. We must avoid stirring up their anger. No, we must be patient and wait. Wait for the end of the war. Wait for Churchill. Wait for Stalin. For some, wait for the Messiah. But others reply that the Messiah has already come. He dines in Berlin with A. H. whose right arm He is. What's happening to us today is in no way related to the Inquisition; then we could have left Spain; we could have converted. Nor with Masada; we could have surrendered, and the Romans didn't pursue an incomprehensible design to exterminate us to the very last, to disinfect the earth of our presence—they couldn't have cared less about our lice. Today even those who have been converted for three generations are marked for extermination. As are Jews who didn't convert even under threat of the sword. And those who chose freely to leave the faith. Even those will die. Even the converts. Even the Jewish police. Even the smugglers. Even the Jewish agents of the Gestapo. They'll be exterminated along with us. We are not, alas, an army of zealots who could surrender to the enemy by waving a humiliating white flag. We are not in a position to abjure our Jewish faith in order to save our lives; Maimonides, according to Reb Huberband, said that was acceptable as long as in your heart you continued to love the Torah of Israel . . .

Szymon was like a madman. Guta kept silent. Szymon is a good man. Esther doesn't deserve him.

○

Esther is reading the works of Napoleon, concentrating mostly on the parts dealing with his last campaigns. Here everyone compares A. H. to Napoleon, speculating endlessly on the similarities and differences between them.

Both made peace with Russia. "Once reconciled with Russia, I will fear no one," said Napoleon. It's certain that A. H. will also know, sooner or later, his Berezina. But between sooner and later, the fate of all Jews hangs in the balance.

Uncle Avrum told her these stories when she was little. He himself heard them from his grandfather, Pinye-Shmulik, a consummate Hasid. It happened in the years 1812–1813, when Napoleon was in the midst of his Russian campaign. Jews, especially Hasidic Jews, were divided into two factions: those who were for Napoleon and those who were for Alexander. The question was whether Napoleon was, in God's plan, the Gog of the land of Magog, of whom the Prophet Ezekiel spoke. On this, they were of two minds. Rabbi Yaakov Yitzhak of Lublin, called the Seer, thought that he was. He had two disciples: one, Rabbi Menachem Mendel of Rymanow, on the side of Napoleon, while the other, Rabbi Yisroel of Kozhenitz, called the Maggid, took the other side. The way the Seer of Lublin reasoned, it was up to the Jews to profit from Napoleon's war in order to hasten the coming of the Messiah.

A fourth Hasid, Rabbi Yaakov Yitzhak of Pzysha, called the Jew, held still another opinion.

Esther remembers that Uncle Avrum would say "even in those days we were already cracked."

In those days then—it was in the summer of 1812 when the Great Army had crossed the Niemen—the Jew from Pzysha had a sort of password with which he greeted everyone, "deliverance is near." When asked what deliverance, he would move away without answering. And when asked the date of its coming, he would say, "it is forbidden to count." Yet, he went everywhere, repeating like a madman, "deliverance is near." And also, I forgot, "time is short."

One day, he visited Rabbi Yisroel of Kozhenitz, the Maggid. The Maggid proclaimed in Kozhenitz the same things as the Jew of Pzysha. But he himself said, "we are turning a corner." Which corner? "*Shalom*, and be in good health," he would say, *zayt mir gezunt*. But the Maggid was obsessed by Napoleon. He hated him, called him the Abominable One. For him, Napoleon was uncontestedly the Gog of the prophet Ezekiel. Let the Jews beware of giving him any aid whatsoever. On the contrary, they should side with Czar Alexander and shout in the face of this Gog demagogue, as it is written in the book of Esther, "You have started to fall, you will fall entirely." For, the Maggid of Kozhenitz maintained, this new Gog would at first be victorious but then his destiny would change. He had this revelation while reading the book of Esther during the last feast of Purim, in early spring of 1812. The Maggid read the fall of the Abominable One in the prediction that Haman's wife made to her own husband that he would "fall." The Maggid didn't know that at that very same moment Napoleon and his Great Army were getting ready to undertake the Russian campaign. Furthermore, it's said that when Prince Poniatowski was warned of Napoleon's intentions, he dispatched his bodyguard, a Jew, to Kozhenitz, and Rabbi Yisroel predicted for him the outcome of the battle.

The Jew of Pzysha was impressed by the Maggid's comments in Kozhenitz. Therefore, to settle the matter once and for all, he decided to talk freely to a declared partisan of Napoleon. So he went to Rymanow to consult Rabbi Menachem Mendel and also to reproach him. "All other peoples," he said, "have armies. They can defend them-

selves, or at least try. But us? We will be like lambs to
the slaughter! And you say that these wars are good for
the Jews. And you support these wars of Napoleon!"

"As long as we can see the end of Exile," answered
Rabbi Menachem Mendel, "it doesn't matter if the fire
also consumes the Jews."

"But," replied the Jew of Pzysha, "how do you know
that the fire is a sign of deliverance? Where did you get
that? Couldn't it simply be our destruction, our annihila-
tion for all time? Do you think that the Messiah will come
into a world devoid of Jews? And who can tell if Napoleon
is indeed this Gog coming from the north with hordes of
soldiers to be decimated in Eretz Ysrael, or if he is the
very Angel of Death?"

Rabbi Mendel kept silent and lowered his eyes. He was
shaken but did not really change his mind.

The Jew took his leave and went back to Pzysha.

They learned of Napoleon's defeat when he retreated
across the Berezina. Some rejoiced, others mourned. The
saddest part of the story was not so much the undoing of
the French Emperor than the fact that nothing had really
changed in the world and in the lives of men. People were
born, people lived, people died as before. This too
needed an interpretation. According to the Jew of Pzysha
it was obvious: it is forbidden to hurry time and to try
to hasten the coming of the Messiah. Certain Hasidim
concluded then that the Messiah would come when people
no longer expected him. But this conclusion didn't satisfy
the Maggid of Kozhenitz. To find out what to make of all
this, he went to Lublin, to consult the Seer. Indeed, said
the latter, they were witnessing the pains of childbirth,
but they had not made ready a crib for the child to be
born; and that is why he was not born.

This is the story that Uncle Avrum told me when I was

little. Today, everyone in the ghetto says that A. H. will also meet his Berezina. Like Napoleon he'll be a ship caught in the ice. And Marshal Stalin will be our Kutusov, the sly fox of the North. Yes, that is certain. But what of the Jews until then?

O

Notices of relocation to the East have been posted on all the ghetto walls. No one can tell me what that means. Rumor has it that a special German commando is to lead this operation. Some say that only nonproductive Jews will be transferred. Yesterday, Germans and Ukrainians surrounded a block of buildings on Niska and Muranowska streets. It seems they need a contingent of six thousand Jews a day. Since they were two thousand short yesterday, they grabbed people at random from buildings on those streets. Then they led them to a place called the *Umschlagplatz*, not far from the Danzig train station.

O

Adam Czerniakow, the president of the Jewish Council, killed himself by swallowing cyanide. He wrote on a block of notepaper left on his table the number "seven thousand." He didn't think of suicide at six thousand. At seven thousand he did. Turn over six thousand Jews, okay. Six thousand Jews led to the *Umschlagplatz*, okay, but seven thousand, oh no, count me out, that's too many. You are insatiable, my friends. There are limits. What will people think?

It was raining cats and dogs yesterday. Today the weather is again like summer.

○

Mathiek came in crying this morning. He had seen how Wladek, Lipshitz's cousin, now with the Jewish police, had beaten those pitiful, exhausted, ragged people. They were groups of refugees who had been expelled from their shelters where they already were dying of hunger. They walked in silence, painfully, followed by trucks into which the Jewish police piled the corpses of those who fell. They were going north on Smocza Street. Mathiek was standing at the corner of Mila. Their probable direction—the *Umschlag*. Why were they singled out for relocation? What use could they be in the East? That's what Mathiek wondered. Esther too. But the answer burst out spontaneously from her mouth, "No use whatsoever. They were being led to their death."

○

Yanek is fine. Esther played with him this morning. He doesn't ask any questions about their parents. Esther avoids talking about them. Besides, she would be incapable of that. There is now this silence between them, this absence.

○

Many Jews are volunteering for "relocation." They claim there is nothing to lose. Their lot there, in this *Pitchipoi* in the East, couldn't be worse than what they're experiencing here. At the *Umschlag*, each volunteer receives three kilos of bread and marmalade. It's a good sign, isn't it?

O

The ceaseless movement of trains, in the Danzig station, where the *Umschlag* leads.

O

Helena Lipshitz died last night. Esther felt guilty about her when she started to weaken, as if she had given her the evil eye. Helena had fainted several times lately, could hardly stand on her feet. Last night, lying on a sofa, she asked Jacob for a glass of tea. When he brought it to her, she looked at him gratefully, took a sip and whispered, "*oy*, this tea is a lifesaver." And then she died, transforming a momentary feeling of well-being into a gruesome joke. For days now she had expressed the wish, rather the folly, to volunteer for the *Umschlag* for the bread and marmalade. Thank God she didn't have the strength to walk there alone.

O

Once again it's Lipshitz's cousin—his ear is everywhere—who warned her. He overheard a conversation in which the name of Dr. Korczak was mentioned. Esther rushed to Yanek's dormitory, took off his uniform, and brought him back to Nowolipie Street.

O

The orphanage was "evacuated." The doctor refused to leave his children. He walked out in front of them carrying a little girl in his arms; the children were singing. Now she must do everything possible to have Yanek pass over to the Aryan sector. But no news of Papa.

O

Some know, others only pretend they know, but most of us keep on wondering: where are these trains going? Are they really used to transport Jews to labor camps inside occupied Russia? Lipshitz has some precise information. According to his Bundist friends, the convoys that leave the *Umschlag* daily don't go very far—only a hundred or so kilometers from Warsaw. To a place called Treblinka. The wagons leaving Warsaw were marked with chalk, and those same marked wagons reappeared on the very same day. Empty. Jews are being massacred in Treblinka. People refuse to believe those rumors because they think that they need us to work and it's not in their interest to kill us. But Esther doesn't know what to think.

O

Szymon and Esther have decided to marry. The very next day. Yes, they'll stand under the canopy. And Szymon will live here.

O

The small ghetto, in the southern part of the Jewish quarter, has been evacuated.

Mrs. Pessakowicz, Szymon's mother, was led to the *Umschlag* and Szymon is going through the phases of deep depression: one minute he's ready to volunteer for death, the next he's seized by the irrational desire for personal revenge. He bought a weapon for its weight in gold. Esther gave him most of the zlotys it took.

Esther will not have children nor will she be a writer. She's tired of thinking only of herself. She is tired of herself. She wonders about the usefulness of her journal. Concludes that it's useless. For those who come after? So that our story will be known. But they know our story. They already know it.

Or do they? Even the Jews don't believe it, still are blind to the fate that awaits them, each one of them. They still think that they can extricate themselves. So this or that member of the Jewish police, who turns his parents in because he thinks it will save his life, participates in the illusion. Because the time will come when it will be his turn to die. What kills us is placing life above all else, *l'chaim*. Treblinka? It's not possible, therefore it's not true. A few months ago, when rumors about what happened in the Chelmno castle reached us, we said the same thing. Jews were reassured, told they were being sent to another ghetto, where men would work in factories, women at housework, and the children would go to school. But before resuming their journey, they had to be disinfected, which meant also their clothing. Therefore, they had to undress, turn over their papers, their valuables. They had to climb into these trucks. And they got undressed and turned over their papers, their jewelry. And they climbed into the big trucks. They couldn't see what followed. They already were gassed. Their corpses were emptied into deep trenches in the woods about ten kilometers from the castle. Rumors, hearsay, the usual Jewish hysteria. Were you there, then how do you know?

They say that in Treblinka there are road signs with the following inscriptions: jewelers, carpenters, shoemakers, tailors, dentists, hairdressers, laundry. What more proof do you need to believe that it's a real labor camp? But they say that the tailor's work is not sewing German uniforms; his work is to collect the uniforms of the deportees, and tie them into bundles to be sent to Germany; that the dentist's job is not taking care of teeth, but to extract gold teeth from the corpses of Jews; that the hairdresser's task is not dressing hair, but to shave the heads of women for their hair. For there, not far from us, at Treblinka, they say that Jews no longer need clothes, gold teeth, jewelry, or hair. None of this is of any use to them.

Get Yanek out of the ghetto. If there is a selection, his fate is sealed: *links*, to the left.

O

A friend of Lipshitz went with another friend to the place where they sort people to try to save I don't know who. They were dressed as doctors and carried a stretcher. The Jews selected for deportation arrived through a door on Stawki Street. Then another selection took place: to the left, to the right. Those not shoved into wagons right away will be deported the next day, or the day after. The Jewish police demand enormous bribes to save people, to get them a white coat, allowing them to mingle with the medical team and come and go among them.

Should there be a selection at our house, Jacob said, his cousin Wladek would warn him. He went ahead and found a hiding place in the loft of a clothing workshop on Smocza Street.

Every night Esther picks up the statue of the tennis player to see what's left of her parent's jewelry. *Klepssidra*, she thinks. They say that at Treblinka that's the

name for those whose faces have been marked by a blow.
Those whose time is measured. Time is measured for all
of us. But for the *Klepssidra* time is measured in hours.
Until the next roll call. Then if they surrender freely, the
SS will be kind, reward their cooperation with a bullet
in the neck, next to the pit prepared for them. But the
others, the malingerers who don't come forth willingly to
their death, or ignore the wound marked on their faces,
once spotted are beaten to death with a shovel.

In the ghetto we are all *Klepssidra*. Esther's hourglass
is her uncle Nathan's *Tennis Player*, Nathan, the sculptor
who went over to Stalin's side. When the statue will be
empty . . .

○

Szymon has found the way to get hold of dosages of
prussic acid. Let him do it without fail. In certain cases,
poison is worth more than gold. Or at least as much.

○

His name is Berl Bronstein. Wladek trusts him completely. He can take Yanek to the Aryan sector. For a
large sum of money because there's considerable risk. He
suggests two possibilities: one is a convent not far from
Warsaw. The risk is that Yanek might become a Catholic.
The other is to place him with a group of children whom
militant Zionists are leading, via Czechoslovakia and Is-
tanbul, to Palestine. The risk is all risk. Esther plans to
speak openly to Berl and ask for his advice.

O

Esther was in a large, verdant, sunny orchard, a dream place where it would be wonderful to live and frolic like a child in lush, welcoming grass. Not far from her, two boys, whom she knows well, are walking. Yes, she knows those two very well. She watches them walking slowly, talking in a low voice; she can't hear and doesn't try to guess what they're saying. On the contrary, she relishes the uninterrupted silence. Next to the orchard, and separated from it by a wire fence, another orchard, an identical one. Suddenly, the neighbor's three dogs cross the "border" and approach her in a gentle, easy, and seemingly casual trot. The first dog is a harmless little poodle; he goes on his way. The next two dogs are German Shepherds. One is a rather old, long-haired dog, with dark fur and dull eyes: he seems not to notice her. The other is a young, short-haired dog with light fur and a thin, muscular, "Aryan" body. He stops in front of Esther, gets ready to pounce, and suddenly executes a magnificent leap, arched like a strained bow, or a rainbow. Esther even has time to admire this leap, this half circle, but not much time because the dog's fangs dig into her and hurt her a lot. The dog's owner, the neighbor, slowly approaches, a worthy fellow dressed like a peasant. He mouths words of advice to Esther, or perhaps hints to his dog rather than commands. But to no avail: Esther's wounds are deep and bleeding. Maybe it's the dog who, not letting her go, dragged her to his owner's house. There she looks for some object along the wall, some garden tool to hold him off. She sees a broom. She tries to pull the dog up to it, but he won't let go of her. Finally she reaches the broom and *lightly* taps the dog with it; eventually he loosens his jaws. But why doesn't Esther smack the dog hard with all her might? Instead (and despite the dog's threats) she turns the broom around, pointing the straw end at the ferocious beast, and taps him on his muzzle. Meanwhile, the pain grows worse and worse.

This morning Esther told Szymon her dream. As for the dogs, he said, the poodle is Poland. The old dog is Russia, the young one is Germany. Besides, there's the regret in Esther of not being a man: she turns the broom around so as to hit the dog with the straw end rather than the hard and "virile" broomstick. But these three dogs, couldn't they also stand for Yanek, Mathiek, and Esther herself? *Nu*, she asked in Yiddish, so? So, nothing, Szymon knows nothing else. Neither does Esther.

O

Esther feels better since getting hold of the acid. The idea that she can end her life, whenever she wants to or must, makes living possible, just barely possible.

A selection took place yesterday in the houses situated between Gesia, Zamenhof, Niska, Smocza, and the other streets near the *Umschlag*. All the inhabitants were ordered to come out. It was six o'clock in the morning. The whole neighborhood was surrounded by the SS, the Ukrainians, and the Latvians. We didn't have to go to our hiding place in the Smocza attic since, for once, the buildings on Nowolipie were spared.

Rabbi Huberband was picked up in the street, just like Mrs. Pessakowicz. Szymon never talks about his mother. He's been given the mission to go from one German factory to another, without a pass, to reestablish the decimated groups of *Hashomer*. Sometimes, when I manage to override his wish to protect me, I go with him. We go at night. Our ghetto has become even more of a fragmented mosaic made up of unconnected little islands fabricated by German workshops, *Klepssidra*.

O

Rosh Hashanah. We're all thinking of the Vistula, which is now off limits to us, where before, groups of pious Jews on that day went to "wash away their sins" by emptying their pockets in the flowing water. Today they can do it in the street. After all, the gutter water runs into the Vistula, doesn't it? There are rumors that in the camp at Oswieçim the Germans spill into the Vistula the ashes of Jews they have burned. After the war, if she survives, how could Esther even think of swimming in this river again?

O

Mathiek is working as a mason. His team oversees the wall, destroys chunks of it, builds it up again. The ghetto keeps on shrinking. Imagine two teams of masons, one working on Okopowa near the cemetery, the other on Bonifraterska. These teams face away from each other. They knock down the wall, then build it up again further inside the ghetto. Sooner or later, the two teams will meet, back to back. By then, the ghetto walls will enclose only a narrow corridor. We'll all have disappeared, except for the masons. It will be child's play for the Germans to make them come out of this corridor, like mice caught in a trap—stupid, inoffensive mice that a child can play with, torture, then deport. They say that in the camps the Germans built in Poland the Jews who handle Jewish corpses are themselves gassed so that no witnesses will survive and tell what they saw. Telling me the story of the

71

Egyptian pyramids when I was a child, Uncle Avrum said that after the Pharaoh's sarcophagus was deposited in his pyramid, the architect and masons were walled up— only they knew the location of the funeral chamber. But what of us, what secret has been deposited with us? The secret of our death—only the one of our death.

O

This morning, on Leszno Street, Esther watched a young man beat a Jewish policeman with his fists. Esther could see him from the rear. He was wearing German boots and a leather windbreaker. A mob had gathered around the combatants; luckily there were no Germans around. Winding her way through the crowd, Esther could see the young man from the front. He was very handsome and fought very well, his punches connecting with his opponent's face. That's what she admired first, even more than his good looks, or that somehow in spite of them, he wasn't afraid to hit with all his might, holding nothing back, aiming straight at his target. Finally, the policeman left, bloodied, yelling insults and threats. Some blackmailing business, the crowd whispered. Esther learned that this young man belonged to a right-wing group of Zionists, the Betar.

Since then, Esther hasn't stopped thinking of him. His name is Akiba Perelstejn. So handsome, so brave! Perhaps in another life Esther will be the lucky lover of such an Akiba? Next to him Szymon doesn't seem very manly. He's only an intellectual. And besides, he doesn't understand anything about literature, or not much. In truth, Esther admits to herself that she doesn't love her husband. She isn't in love with him. She's fond of him, that's all. She respects him. She's grateful to him for loving her.

Because at least she's sure of his feelings toward her. Sure also that he'll be able to protect her, or would be able. In a normal world and life, he would have been able to take care of her, to want a child by her. Now he doesn't even think about it.

Even in the midst of disaster I'm still waiting for a great passion, a real passion. Yes, madness. I need madness. Let the world be ordered but give me a madness that is mine, that belongs to me alone. Here, in our ghetto streets, madness surrounds us, assaults us more and more each day. But that's the madness of the world, not mine. I want my own, I have a right to it.

Helena's death didn't affect her. She saw in it a chance for Jacob to consider her differently from now on, as a woman. How could she communicate her desire to him? Jacob is, was, very attached to his wife. And then there's also Szymon. The two men meet every day, are friends, at least so it seems. Esther will die without ever having been in love. She admires Jacob. Recently he agreed to recite his poems to her; they're not extraordinary, that she can't deny. But the way he recites them! He seems so handsome then. There's such strength emanating from his face and his body! She would be ready to do anything. In her daydreams she mistakes him for the young man from Betar who is such a good fighter. Jacob would fight like this even though he's no longer a young man. Does she dare to speak to him? She must. It's possible. It's allowed. We're all going to die. Our days are numbered. But to betray Szymon? Do this to him when death is so close, two steps away, two days? And he loves her so much.

They say that only fifty thousand Jews are left in the ghetto. This summer alone, they "transferred" more than three hundred thousand. The prophet Isaiah predicted it: "Barely a tenth will survive and they, in turn, will be destroyed."

○

Yom Kippur. Mathiek has disappeared. He had the right ID papers, but that's small comfort. I dread the worst. Poor Martha Lipshitz is beside herself.

○

Esther is too kind. She suggested to Martha that she work with them in *Hashomer*. The group agreed and found her a job in Schultz Enterprises. She seems to have made a conquest of Lev, a comrade who's over thirty years old. New couples come and go surprisingly fast. Is Mathiek ashes for her already? What really bothers Esther is that frivolous, scatterbrained Martha is now considered her equal in the movement; it's as if she'd been a member forever. Szymon keeps telling her that they need all the help they can get, but in vain . . .

○

Last night, at two in the morning, some men came for Yanek. They were friends of Wladek. They all went down the stairs in silence. Esther held her brother's trembling little hand. As they walked through the streets, she wondered if she had made the right decision. Would he get all the way to Palestine? Probably not. But she had no other choice. They arrived at the wall. Esther thought of her father, of the times she played with Yanek, and of the silence between them about Freydla's disappearance. A ladder stood against the wall, the top of which was spread with broken glass on top. One of the men covered the glass with a blanket for protection. They had to hurry and didn't have time to say goodbye. Suddenly Esther no longer felt Yanek's hand in her own. He was already climbing the ladder, until it disappeared after him. And then a man who had stayed behind was tugging at her sleeve, signaling for them to return. He went with her as far as Nowolipie, and told her in a low voice that she'd have to pay the sum they agreed on in two days, when the boy would be safe in the Aryan Zone.

O

Last night in our bed, I don't know why, or rather I do—because of the other night's dream—I told Szymon of something that happened in my childhood. I was barely ten years old, perhaps even younger. We lived on Bonifraterska Street in those days. That particular evening we had invited our friends, Mr. and Mrs. Goldberg, a rich, refined couple, and Uncle Avrum and his wife, Toba. Maybe it was the eve of *Shabbes*. After dinner Esther played with Adek on the sofa. She stroked his hair; he still had a headful then. She tangled and untangled his hair, massaged it, combed it, recombed it. Adek let her do it; he liked it. Then Esther grew tired of the game, stopped, and started to yawn. Adek told her to put her hand in front of her mouth. He told her the story of a little girl who, yawning as she did, dislocated her jaw. That frightened Esther, who asked him to explain. How did the jaw become dislocated? How was that possible? And since right away she started to yawn again, Adek suddenly, inexplicably, to surprise her, to make her stop yawning or maybe simply in play, stuck a finger in her

mouth, and rather deeply inside. Esther stopped yawning. And not knowing why, perhaps because she was insulted—but why insulted?—she bit her father's index
finger, holding it as long as possible firmly between her
teeth. Szymon said that it was because she wanted to *keep*
his finger in her mouth, inside of her always, because she
didn't want to grow old, grow up, and leave Adek, give
up the idea of being his wife . . . And when she finally
let go of her father's finger, Adek seemed to be in intense
pain—it had really hurt him—and he looked at his sore
finger and, unexpectedly, slapped her. What did Szymon
think? Nothing, he didn't have an opinion. He was tired
and wanted to sleep. He turned over. It was when he was
snoring that Esther realized that this wasn't her memory,
wasn't her memory at all. It was the opposite. It was he,
Adek, who had yawned. And it was she, Esther, who had
put her finger in her father's mouth. And it was he who
had bitten it, bitten her very hard. No, she had not
slapped him. The idea had never occurred to her.

O

Laikin, the commissar of the Jewish police, along with
Firth, a functionary of the *Judenrat*, have been liquidated by our comrades.

The other night Jacob recited a love poem for us but
refused to say who wrote it. Since the poem didn't sound
familiar, I concluded that it was one of his own. I'm sure
that he thought of me while writing and reciting it. He
wrote it for me; he recited it for me. I tried to meet his
eyes the other night but could not. Clearly, he made sure
that our gazes wouldn't meet; it's a sign, isn't it? As if he
feared something, a confession revealed to the others or
to myself. He must feel guilty about Helena's memory,

and also about Szymon. Me too. He must be in love with me. What a hell for him! At night, Szymon no longer takes me in his arms. He's tired. He turns away with a distressing *oy*, a sigh of a drowning man, and falls asleep right away, even on nights when the sound of gunshots prevents the rest of us from sleeping. Not him. Nothing prevents him from sleeping. Some people are made that way. That's my husband. Without whom I'd be alone.

O

At first they thought of sending Szymon, in the name of *Zydowska Organizacja Bojowa* (ZOB), the organization of Jewish fighters, to negotiate for weapons on the Aryan side. But in the end, Esther doesn't know why, Jacob was picked to go. The first ten guns obtained from the Polish Resistance were hidden in small wooden boxes in a handcart pushed by a Pole, a certain Stefan Pokropek. For a few zlotys, a Polish policeman on Dzika Street agreed to close his eyes, thinking it was the usual smuggled goods.

What struck Esther in all this was the name of the Polish partisan, Pokropek. A long time ago, when she was perhaps eight years old, she had gone to fetch Adek from his hat shop, and they had walked home together from Praga. Adek was holding her hand. They crossed the Saxon Gardens, then at the corner of Orla and Leszno, Adek stopped and shook hands with a policeman. Usually, when Adek met a friend or Freydla a crony and they stopped to chat, Esther would grow impatient, and grumble, and would pull them by the sleeve. But now, Adek standing before this Polish policeman with big aristocratic mustaches, shaking hands as though they were old acquaintances—when the Litvaks never associated with Poles—Esther was dazzled. Just think of Daddy shaking hands with a Pole! and a policeman no less! and in uniform! She couldn't believe her eyes. She was overcome by boundless admiration for him, her chest swelling not with pride but because suddenly she couldn't catch her breath and felt like crying. And on the way home, she asked him a flood of questions: Who was he? How did he know him? What was his name? Since when had they been friends? Adek answered all these questions in a self-confident and evasive manner, himself no less proud, hoping that a Jewish acquaintance would happen by, and seeing him, burst with surprise and envy. Esther had forgotten the substance of the conversation, but she remembers questioning her father also about the way he had spoken to the Pole, choosing his words, picking the prettiest, the rarest ones, all without the slightest Yiddish accent, without a hint of Yiddish intonation, speaking the Polish of Poles and not theirs, the Polish of Jews, a substandard mix that earned them mocking, even cruel, remarks from the Catholics. She still remembers his name, Pokropek, and his big, red, walrus mustache that he twisted into corkscrew curls like those of the Hasidim.

O

Lipshitz is going to be sent to the Aryan Zone. He told me that he'd try to see Papa. If he's still alive. I'm very much afraid that he won't come back, that something will happen to him. He is to leave in two days. I must speak to him before that. I notice that more and more I prefer to call him Lipshitz instead of the usual Jacob. Calling him by his last name gives him a certain prestige. Especially that last name, Lipshitz, *protected lips*, which fits him so well.

○

Last night Esther turned down Szymon's offer to go with him to visit some *Hashomer* comrades. His surprise was obvious but he didn't ask questions. Perhaps it was better that way. What did he mean by that? All in all, he doesn't mind going by himself. But why?

Jacob got some potatoes and, using for fuel the arm of a chair he found in the building's courtyard, cooked them in the kitchen oven. They were alone in the apartment, a situation Jacob seemed to find amusing and probably pleasant. Esther should have thrown herself in his arms. He wouldn't have pushed her away, of that she's sure. Why would he refuse a girl like her, well, a young woman? On the contrary, he would have kissed her, as though he'd been waiting a long time, a very long time, but hadn't dared say anything. Protected lips, right? Instead, Esther spoke about his next mission, but after a while he came up to her, put a finger against her mouth, whispered "shhh!" and stared at her. At that moment she should have . . . But what of Szymon, Helena, all that? . . . And what of herself? Because it's the man who should make the first move. What does it mean to want someone—to want a man? That, she believes, has never happened to her. Never before Jacob. Thinking about him, she feels something like a pain in her gut. Nothing like that with Szymon, ever. Jacob has something of an Errol Flynn. And even Johnny Weismuller. Tarzan! She's in love with a Tarzan! Here! In the ghetto! In this jungle-ghetto! At the same time she feels the need to speak to Szymon, to tell him all this. A mistake, that would be a great mistake. A fatal one.

○

Jacob left. Esther confessed. Spoke. Since then, she
can't sleep. She can't stop crying. Szymon looks at her
as she cries, silent, distressed, not understanding. Does
she want them to separate? She says no. Did she tell him
that she doesn't love him anymore? Maybe, she thinks
so. Did she really say those words: "I don't love you anymore, Szymon, I don't love you anymore"? He asks her
again if she wants to separate. She says no. Szymon also
starts crying: only now does he realize that his mother's
in Treblinka, and that she is ashes. They cry together,
each for himself, each alone. Szymon wants to say something, but can't talk. He says "Treblinka." He says the
word, only the word. Then they talk of the tractors that
bury the corpses there, or the ash of corpses, the corpses
that have become ash. He says that his mother was the
last old woman in the ghetto. She was forty-five. Last
summer, says Esther, nobody did a thing to prevent the
deportations. On some days, at the *Umschlag*, they
turned people away because there were so many volunteers. All for a little bread! Other days, when their quota
hadn't been reached, it was our own police that rounded
up the Jews, led them to the *Umschlag*, pushed them into
the wagons. And in Treblinka they say that it's the Jews
themselves who . . . Szymon knew that . . . did the
work, . . . He knew that . . .

○

"The book of Esther says that all of King Ahasuerus'
servants would kneel and bow to Haman because the king

had ordered it—all, that is, but Mordecai who neither knelt nor bowed." So, continued Uncle Avrum, the king's order was a tragic dilemma for Mordecai. A Talmudic rabbi had these comments about it: "The people of Israel spoke to the Blessed be He and said: 'Master of the Universe, the idolaters are setting a trap to catch me; they push me to prostrate myself before their idols. If I obey them, you will punish me; if I disobey them, they will kill me.'" This is the dilemma, Uncle Avrum went on, either Mordecai kneels before Haman and breaks the Law of God, and God punishes him—maybe by condemning him to death—or Mordecai refuses to bow, and it is the whole Jewish race that risks being exterminated. And that rabbi, Rabbi Yosi Bar Hanina, went on to say that it was like a wolf dying of thirst for whom a trap has been set near the river. The wolf says: "If I go to drink, I'll be captured, if I don't, I'll die of thirst."

According to Uncle Avrum, the water of the river represented the Torah and the trap the prohibition imposed on Jews to study it. But no matter. This condemned wolf stuck in Esther's mind; this wolf is condemned to a sure death, no matter what he does or doesn't do. And these days she thinks about it more and more. Because in the past our enemies gave us a choice: we could convert, renounce our faith, or die. Today, no. We're in the same situation as the thirsty wolf of Rabbi Yosi Bar Hanina, either way destined to die. Some people in the ghetto still believe in their own luck, thinking that, like Haman in the Book of Esther, the Germans will flip coins—their life or their death. They forget that Haman was Oriental, and enjoyed gambling and irony. Not the Germans. The Germans are not gamblers. They don't consult the fates. They decide and they execute. And they have decided.

Nothing will prevent them from acting, neither their victory, of course, nor their defeat. Because when Stalin, Roosevelt and Churchill defeat them—and they will defeat them—we will no longer exist, and from the ash of our corpses flowers will have grown.

○

The deportations started up again last night. No news of Mathiek. An icy wind is blowing and it's begun to snow. Hannah Krawetz brought me a book about French literature that she found under a porch on Mylna Street. Its title is *La Littérature française du brevet élémentaire et de l'enseignement primaire supérieur*. These words make me dream. The book is thick, slightly dog-eared, with beautiful red covers. On the flyleaf is written the motto, "As you sow, so shall you reap." I can't, alas, read this book but I spend hours leafing through it, waiting for Lipshitz to return; he went to negotiate for weapons in the Aryan Zone. How did this book wind up here, in Warsaw? Perhaps a young Jew who had emigrated to France returned to visit his family on Mylna Street. Did he get out in time? Is he already dead?

○

Lipshitz came back, Thank God! He put on weight again. The comrades are pleased: the Pfefer tannery on Okopowa Street will deliver the "merchandise." Esther made a date with him, and they met in the loft of the clothing workshop on Smocza Street. Esther loved him and she didn't care about Szymon. She no longer loved her husband, in fact, had never loved him. She wanted to make it with Jacob. They would find a way, perhaps here, in this loft. Jacob was willing. But he wanted her to think it over: Szymon was a friend, a devoted comrade. And then she couldn't count on him, ever, she should realize that. He promised her nothing. Besides, she should know that he had had two affairs in the Aryan Zone. With whom? With some Jewish women working as servants for Poles and living under false identities. He meant to keep his freedom. What freedom? Esther screamed. She knew at once that she had no right, no right to scream, no rights over him. But he was right. She would think it over. She neither could nor wanted to betray Szymon; too many things bound her deeply to him. She left first—they had agreed that Jacob would wait ten minutes before coming down himself.

Once in the street she realized that she was being inconsistent in saying that she didn't want to betray Szymon. The harm was done; she had betrayed him. Ah, you are worthless, kiddo, less than worthless. Maybe she could fix things by telling him everything, the meeting with Lipshitz, what she said, what he said, everything. And Szymon wouldn't . . .

It was then that she witnessed a horrible scene at the corner of Smocza and Nowolipki. A German soldier was speaking in a friendly way to a Jew, which surprised her and made her slow down to watch. As she came closer, she saw the German take out his gun and shoot another Jew whom she hadn't noticed, but who was walking nearby, not on the sidewalk but in the street—he had removed his cap. Then the German, still smiling at his Jew, shot that Jew also, in the belly, as if the first bullet had merely whetted his appetite and he was still a little hungry for murder. When the Jew fell to the ground, the soldier shot him again in the head. And then burst out laughing. Esther stared at the ground, afraid that something terrible would happen to her, but she was able to continue on her way.

At home Szymon was waiting for her. Where had she been? She had just had a tête-à-tête with Jacob. Szymon didn't respond, stopped asking questions, and went back to reading the thick book by Darwin. Explanations were superfluous.

Esther began to sing a Yiddish tune, happy—yes, happy—that Lipshitz hadn't turned her down. Suddenly she started to cry. What was wrong with her? She didn't know, didn't know why she was crying. And Szymon came over to her.

O

She told Hannah everything. Hannah told her not to hesitate, to take up with Jacob. Esther doesn't think she means it: Hannah isn't really putting herself in her place. Besides, Hannah is not in her place. Perhaps she harbors some perverse desire to see Szymon and Esther separate. Her own love affair hadn't withstood the war, and she's jealous, happy to see the undoing of another couple; it's some sort of consolation to her. She now says that a woman, in the twentieth century, must be a man's equal, must live freely and have all sorts of adventures. We must abandon the old morality, the morality of our mothers and its sinister retinue of faithfulness, devotion, sacrifice. She doesn't mean it.

O

Jacob looked for Papa in the vicinity of Praga but couldn't find him. Nor did he find anyone who could supply any information about him. No news either of Yanek. Nor of Mathiek.

Meanwhile, in the ghetto, we create hiding places. We reinforce cellars, wall up attics, fit cupboards inside other cupboards, build real trapdoors and fake trapdoors into the floor, then cover them up with rugs, or with tables, carve out real stairs and fake stairs. And we do even better: we build fake rooms. Blind, windowless, doorless rooms whose walls are reinforced by several layers of brick, with no access except though the roof, by removing tiles. Blind rooms are built into other blind rooms! Engineers, mechanics pitch in with their precious expertise. Some have even turned it into a living. A new trade—selling hiding places. The price of the contract includes food. Many of the survivors pass over to the Aryan side for colossal sums of money. They don't believe in hiding places. They say they're all known to the Germans—because they're known to the Jews, thus to Jewish informers. What they refuse to consider is that once on the Aryan side they'll live with the constant fear of being denounced. When their money or jewelry runs out, the Poles who hid them for a while won't think twice about turning them over to the Germans. Profit insured—a hundred zlotys per head. Those who remain in the ghetto are resolved to die weapon in hand. They stock up on food. It's no longer a question of hiding for a night or during a roundup, but for weeks, months perhaps, until the final assault.

O

The League of Nations has condemned the extermination of the Jews. It even went so far as to threaten the Nazis with punishment. This will surely dissuade them from continuing. They're so sensitive to threats, especially coming from such a respectable lady as the League of Nations.

A thick layer of snow covers the streets. Under the pavement, blood—streams of it.

○

At night Esther sees her little brother among the group of Janusz Korczak's children. Led by the doctor who carries a little girl in his arms, the children are proceeding in the direction of the *Umschlag*. Yanek is smiling, and like the other children, he is singing, and suddenly his smile freezes into a horrible grimace and his song turns into cacophony, screams in which Esther can distinguish *rechts*, *links*, right, left. And the dogs are showing their fangs.

Every night she has these nightmares.

It's snowing.

Treblinka.

She's moving in a few hours. She'll be staying in a shelter on Smocza Street. For the time being she doesn't want to stay with Szymon. She told him so. She needs to get away, get some distance from him in order to see things more clearly. She told him that, too. As she wishes. If she wishes. He never says anything else.

○

Szymon accompanied Esther to Smocza Street. When he left he told her, "I think you're doing all this to test me, to see if I'll beg you to stay with me, to see whether or not I love you, and to see how long I'm willing to go on insisting, imploring you, and if I'll make a scene. Well, don't count on me for those games. I have other things to do, much more important than this stupid nonsense, this *narishkayt* . . ."

Always when he's angry or else very tender he uses Yiddish words. Esther is rather fond of him at these moments. Lipshitz, on the other hand, uses Yiddish words when he's trying to establish collusion, and he uses them in the wrong way, or makes mistakes.

Szymon doesn't love me anymore, that's all. Here's the big news. The big news in the ghetto. Even if the speech he made was only feigned and forced on his part, even if he made it only through bravado, through ego, it is no less startling for Esther to hear. Where does this sudden strength come from, if not from the fact that he no longer loves her? Perhaps he's already secretly in love with this redhead, this fast woman who hangs around their kibbutz on Mila Street? Secretly, that is, he doesn't know it yet himself. . . . I dread the worst: to lose Szymon and have Jacob reject me in the long run. The truth is that she's not Jacob's equal. He's capable of seducing any woman, Jewish or Christian. And she, Esther, what is she capable of? Is she going to play the *femme fatale*? He'd see that she's acting, and doing a bad job of it. She who weighs less than a hundred pounds, with her baby face, how could she compete with busty redheads? According to Hannah—where does she get her information, from what previous life or studies?—men like to show off with slim, supple-bodied women, but their deep instinct drives them to sensual women with big breasts and buttocks, like their mother's. A little sister satisfies them for a while but they soon feel the need for a second mother. . . *azoy*, so that's the way it is . . .

○

Rumors announce the imminent resumption of deportations. Are we ready to resist them? Most say no. There's a grievous lack of money, so we're reduced to ransoming the rich and the members of the *Judenrat*.

○

German *Aktion* started up again yesterday morning with unprecedented brutality. The ghetto was locked at dawn. But we counterattacked! Esther joined a group of about forty fighters in a kibbutz on Zamenhof Street. Among them was the poet Katzenelson cheering on the comrades, saying that he was happy to die at their side, weapon in hand. He had come with his son. The comrades advised him to take cover because the Germans were expected any moment: it was important that he survive at any cost, in order to bear witness. But he refused.

○

Today is the fourth day of the German *Aktion*. Terrible explosions can be heard: they blow up houses, throw grenades into apartments. The roundups have stopped. The Germans are no longer trying to deport, but to kill as many Jews as possible, in revenge. The Polish underground is still as stingy as ever with weapons. When I think of all the time wasted in cultural activities when we should have been training to fight. But we didn't know, not knowing A. H.

○

Uncle Avrum used to tell me that on the third day of creation, when steel was created, the trees began to tremble. What's the matter with you that you tremble so? asked the steel. Let none of you serve me as a handle, and you'll have nothing to fear from me. In this fable, according to Avrum, the trees represent Israel prostituted before the nations, and the steel the nations' seductive force. And when Israel serves as a handle for the steel of nations, he added, the nations become axes, mercilessly chopping down the trees of Israel.

Here in the ghetto, we finally seem to have understood this fable. We'll no longer be used as handle for the steel that strikes us. But it's a bit late to be opening our eyes.

O

It's only too obvious that Lipshitz doesn't want me. He tries to avoid me. Deep down, he's indifferent to me. My "declaration" had no effect on him. Perhaps he thinks it's only a passing fancy on my part, that I'm just an infatuated adolescent who'll soon recover her wits. Szymon must think the same thing. Otherwise he wouldn't react the way he does, that is, he'd react. Unless there's already in him a silent, unconscious process of distancing at work. He no longer desires me. Lipshitz never desired me, except in my dreams. There I confuse him with the Adek of my youth. A strong creature, even violent and brutal. Szymon also reminds me of my father. But of my father today—a compulsive man, unsure of himself. Also a somewhat feminine man, rather passive, contemplative. A man who *waits*.

We are all dying.

Each night Esther goes through the ritual of making sure the acid under the *Tennis Player* hasn't disappeared. This gives her the strength to go on for another day. To put off until the next day the idea of ending it all. Then again to the next day.

○

It's been three days since Lipshitz was sent to the Aryan Zone. It was arranged that a Pole would telephone on his behalf that very evening, but we've heard nothing. That he deserted like Papa is out of the question. Or a Polish woman? No, he was caught. Followed, denounced, brought to the police station, turned over to the Germans. She can't find the strength to swallow the acid.

○

Szymon ignores me. From now on I'm a stranger to him. I'm dragging around my life for nothing and for no one. I'll turn myself in, let myself be led to the *Umschlag*. I won't bury these sheets of papers deep in the ground so that maybe one day they'll be found. Nor will I entrust them to Hannah, who's leaving tomorrow and forever for the Aryan Zone, preferring—and she's right—the risk of living to the certainty of dying.

Destroy, destroy, these are the only words that still hold meaning for me. And I hardly understand them. But there's no time left.

Destroy, destroy. Everyone has his task: they, the Mongols, my life; me, Esther Litvak, my journal. To each one his task. Napoleon said it well: mud, that's all there is. Poland is mud. Mud is Poland. Left, right, stand up, fall down. The seventh time, the walls came tumbling down. By the wounds of Christ! Ptachia Street herring. It's not my fault, it's the herring of Ptachia Street! Shhhh! Lipshitz, protected lips. I'll never have children, ever. My little doll, that's what he used to call me. *Liulilke, mein kind.* The walls are tumbling down. Stand up, fall down. The prophet Elijah sits at A. H.'s dinner table. They say he's his right arm. As strong as Joshua. A better *shofar,* much better. The Jews themselves are producing it. They work hard, the Jews, when they need to. Steel and trees. And dogs. Dogs everywhere. And rats too, in all the courtyards, in all the cellars. Fanciers of corpses. But the dogs, especially. Where is my doll? Lialka. Like the SS chief of Treblinka. He has his dog. Bari, that's his name. A handsome dog name. Really handsome name. Me, he won't bite. Not bite Esther. Esther bite German Shepherd Bari. Bite Adek?

II

The necrophore is a coleopter beetle that buries carrion, cadavers of moles and mice, on which it lays its eggs.

Le Petit Robert

1

A Dream

They're all there, in full force. Mama Bear, Papa Bear, daughter Bear, and the two cubs. And they're going home. Their street is on the other side of the crossroads. They're standing at the edge of the sidewalk. Papa Bear looks out for traffic. There are police vans parked all about. Now they cross the street to reach the opposite sidewalk. And right away the policemen get out of their vans, aim their guns and shoot. Mathieu feels like a target. But he's wrong, they're shooting at dogs, yes dogs, German Shepherds, abandoned German Shepherds. Roaming, disoriented.

The policemen are wearing strange helmets. They look like Nazi helmets. That's just what they look like.

There are two German Shepherds lying in their path, barring the door to the apartment. The dogs are a couple. Mathieu, who walks in front of his parents, doesn't dare step over the two dogs. He's not afraid of them, that's not it, he even feels a little sorry for them; he's well aware of the fate the "Germans" have in store for them in the street. That's because the Litvaks themselves also own two dogs—which is curious—two rather imposing dogs, of a different breed from German Shepherds, their fur much longer, the head much friendlier.

Papa Bear moves ahead of his oldest son, steps over the two apathetic dogs, and, as he opens the door, the male dog growls a little. Nothing serious.

Hanging back, Mathieu plays with one of the Litvak dogs. The animal has enormous canine teeth. He doesn't snap at Mathieu's hand—it's Mathieu who, in spite of himself, sticks his hand into those jaws. And it hurts a lot. Even though Mathieu taps the dog on the muzzle, the dog doesn't let go. Mathieu taps him harder, and he finally lets go of the hand and gives him his paw.

Mathieu runs to his room, to his childhood desk and opens a drawer. It's jammed with relics of Nazi camps, crammed in the way that children accumulate disparate objects. But he can make out only the naked body of a torn doll. He concludes a little sadly that he hasn't yet accumulated many objects. His collection is rather skimpy, inadequate. When he closes the drawer, part of the doll's body sticks out. He closes it again, and the doll's arm or leg still sticks out. He turns away from the desk. There's a piece of paper conspicuous on the mantle, with a child's drawing that Mathieu knows came from a Nazi camp. This doll's limb sticking out really bothers him.

And scares him. And wakes him up. He remembers then that Lalka was a nickname for Kurt Franz, one of the SS in Treblinka. He had a vicious dog, Bari. And that *lialka* is the Yiddish word for doll. And he feels a host of other things rising in him, but he falls asleep again.

The Photograph

It's been decreed: Esther is the "brain" of the family. It's been decided; let's not bring it up again. Mathieu and Yanick must do the best they can. It doesn't matter. Esther is the only one who really counts, that's the way it is. It's in the nature of things. And, besides, the most important thing is to be well adjusted. Too much education, too much reading. Esther is "sick." It's settled, let's not bring it up again. She is "sick."

At home, the "library" is in the bathroom—basically, three small shelves. Some Communist and Soviet literature, a few Communist and Soviet novels. That's enough for the time spent going to bathrooms. The music corner is in the living room, next to the record-player: Red Army choruses, Yves Montand, 78-rpm tangos, paso dobles in Yiddish, scratched long-playing albums missing their jackets, all in careless piles.

Esther has her own books, her own records, no one's allowed to touch them. She is a gifted student. She wants to become a teacher, later on. "Sick" as she is, she will succeed. Gifted, yes. Yet Charles and Fanny don't brag about her, ever. Something in her remains closed to them, a total lack of understanding, a painful mystery, a punishment from the good Lord. What exactly did they do wrong? They wonder. The war, says Charles, it's the war's doing. Nothing can be done.

On the wall of her room Esther has pinned up the photograph of women fighters in the Warsaw Ghetto, young women in rags and wearing caps, lined up, probably facing a firing squad. You can't see the firing squad. But they are lined up. And it's the Germans who took this picture. Therefore they must be facing a firing squad. This photograph has always been up on the wall near Esther's bed. Still there today. No one thought of removing it, or thought of it and didn't dare. It is fitting that it stay there, after all. The picture is moving. And, besides, this photograph is really Esther. It evokes Esther. It's a little as if she were still there among them. Charles and Fanny didn't see the point of removing it, either after their daughter's marriage or her death.

Born on . . . in . . .

Whenever Mathieu goes to visit his parents, he rushes to his sister's room without anyone knowing. He stands in front of the photograph. He tries to understand. He concentrates, but his mind grows confused, and it doesn't take long for his head to feel empty. But he stays in front of the picture as though collecting his thoughts. On Esther's desk, next to her notebooks and a few books, there sat, until Mathieu snatched it, the cap that Charles and Fanny kept of her, the cap that she bought herself and wore in the streets. She looked ridiculous; it was embarrassing to see her in it. She was trying to look like one of these young women in the picture. Each time he is in his sister's room, after making sure that he's alone, Mathieu tries on the cap. It is much too big for him, as it must have been for his sister. And he quickly puts it back in its place, as if he were committing a sacrilege. He would wonder about the photograph's date. By the time Esther was born, there hadn't been a ghetto in Warsaw for months. All that was left there was rubble, rubble. When Esther was born, the ghetto was little more than a field of rubble. Born too late, and on top of it, on the wrong meridian. How do you make up for two mistakes? When Esther was born, the Jews of Warsaw had been exterminated, all of them. She had missed a train. So she set her watch back on time, to the time of that train's departure. One fine day in the spring of 1975, she stuck her head into her oven. When her husband came home from work, he found her dead. Not the least explanation, no note. At least, none were found. For Mathieu, Esther's goodbye letter was the photograph in her old room, and the oversized cap sitting on her desk. She probably bought it in some flea market. She loved browsing in flea markets, looking for unpromising old things, relics from the past, like evidence.

Charles and Fanny were quite repulsed by the cap but didn't dare throw it out. A letter of goodbye would have been superfluous. Her act did not really surprise anyone. As if it were expected, expected because it was so dreaded. Even Yanick must have understood the whole business.

Mathieu and Yanick had been offered life on a platter. Not Esther. It was as if she were guilty of being alive. She had to earn this "luck," this misfortune. Charles and Fanny felt guilty, in turn, responsible for their eldest daughter's unhappiness.

Esther used to stand in front of her mirror wearing this ridiculous and oversized cap. How many times did they surprise her in this pose, trying hard to suppress their smiles? A girl her age, look at her still playing like a child? And screaming insults, she would slam the door right in their faces. And, then and there, outside the door to her room, they would burst out laughing. Hunched over, face flushed, head between his shoulders, Charles would put his finger against his open mouth roaring like a tiger, *Shhhh!*

Esther frightens Mathieu. When he's near her, he's afraid of being contaminated. He feels he must protect himself. He protects himself with blindness and deafness, he sees no other way. Simon Pessakowicz, her husband, isn't as complicated. You can talk to him. To Esther, you cannot. She's locked behind the ghetto wall, unattainable. And why not write a novel about the Warsaw Ghetto? Since it's her obsession. There's an idea! Bunch of morons, she says. Just morons. But why is the idea so crazy? Yes, why, let her explain. Bunch of morons, that's what they are. Fine.

Perhaps she's already writing this novel on the sly. And that's what disturbs her so much. Better not insist.

Mathieu has forgotten Esther since her death. They have all forgotten her. In any case, they never speak about her. She is taboo. Her old room remains untouched, like a memorial. Mathieu stands in front of the photograph. But it's not familiar to him. It doesn't ring a bell, doesn't remind him of anything. However hard he searches his memory, nothing. So he returns to the family circle.

What's there to say about Esther? What's there to add? Everything has been said. She herself has said everything. Even Simon doesn't speak of it. As Mathieu thinks it over, Simon took no time at all to remarry. . . . As if he had to rectify an error, correct a misunderstanding, right away . . .

West Beirut = Warsaw Ghetto

In the beginning of the summer of 1982 the Israeli army went into Lebanon. The newspapers spoke of the Warsaw

Ghetto. Well, the newspapers are very cultured! They know their history. Beirut, where the PLO army was entrenched, was *like* the Warsaw Ghetto. That's obvious, indeed. Soon they refined it: they stopped saying "like." They eliminated the "like." Beirut *was* the Warsaw Ghetto. Not like. Was. And the Palestinians? The Jews of the ghetto. And the Israelis? The Nazi army. It all fit well together, a marvelous conjuring trick. Were they lying in good faith or in ignorance? Were they lying by design? That summer Mathieu missed Esther. He wouldn't have hesitated to give her a call, and this time they could have talked. But she wasn't there anymore. She was dead. Esther was dead, and Mathieu realized it that summer when the Israeli army went into Lebanon. And when the newspapers spoke of the ghetto. There were even Jews who spoke of the ghetto. Who omitted the *like*. That was the most unbearable part, these Jews serving as handle for the steel ax, that same ax that would strike them, that already was striking them that summer, and meanwhile they yelled with the others, *Israel* = *Nazi!*

The Rats

Mathieu's life flows like a river, widening, almost without meandering. He works for a government agency. He knows that his position is not really brilliant. You would have thought he had to apologize for it to his parents. Not at all, they say; as for "brilliant," we already gave. There's been enough "brilliant" in their life; that will do. They don't want any more "brilliant." What they aspire to, from now on, is some "normal," nothing but "normal." No "brilliant." No more "brilliant," thank you. At least with the government, says Charles, Mathieu won't have any slow season. Oh, does he think that there's a fast season in the office? That's it, let him complain! He doesn't realize how lucky he is. The life they knew in Poland is over, once and for all, a life of *pariahsites*. To be a civil servant in France, that's ideal!

Mathieu deploys his talents in a crammed office, a cramped nook on the seventh floor of a large building. It can be reached by one of four elevators. Mathieu doesn't always choose the same one; it depends on his mood, on whether or not he feels like exploring a new corner, or encountering new faces—feminine perhaps. He even had the strange idea that, one time or other, he would run into a rat scurrying around the corner of a hallway. Fear or wish, he couldn't say. Perhaps a wish. He dreamed that all of it would be gnawed away, little by little, this large building with tons of papers and files; but gnawed away slowly, imperceptibly, so that no one could tell. Only he would have noticed. He would guard this secret preciously in his heart of hearts; he would measure the infinitesimal progress of the damage every day, the faint, less and less faint, bite marks at the foot of a door, on top of a cabinet, chair, table. But he never saw the slightest rat. And no trace whatsoever of bites.

The Grave

Mathieu is rather fond of the cemetery in Bagneux where his sister is buried. She's interred in the Jewish section, with the other family members, those who died normal deaths. On her tombstone there also appear the slightly old-fashioned medallion-portraits of the others, those whose bodies are not there, whose bodies lie elsewhere, whose bodies no longer exist, whose bodies are scattered, dissolved in rivers, the Bug, the Vistula, or are mixed with the earth, well mixed, as ash and earth can be mixed, then raked clean. Most of all, raked clean.

There are three portraits, one for the "other" Esther, Fanny's sister, one for Rivka Tenenbaum, one for Raisl Litvak. The first two died in Auschwitz, the third in Treblinka. It's all spelled out on the gravestone. All you have to do is read.

Mathieu always liked cemeteries. It's no easy thing to walk around in them. There are holes in the ground as numerous as the holes in Swiss cheese. You could fall in at any moment and become trapped. The Jewish cemeteries are especially moving, or rather, the Jewish sections of certain cemeteries. Perhaps because death seems less commonplace there. It's ridiculous, obviously. But Jewish death, even the ordinary kind, is never a small matter to him. He's tempted to respect it more than the other kind, to be more moved by it. The other kind, that is, the ordinary, everyday kind. Even ordinary Jewish death is never entirely ordinary in his eyes. It's always like the carbon copy, the duplicate of another death, not ordinary, a death that means that your corpse doesn't last long as a corpse. The immediate burning of the corpse—as if one didn't quite know what to do with it—is very burdensome, isn't it? As is the fact that the gathered ashes are never quite gathered but dispersed, mixing with the earth, the good, fertile, Polish earth, or thrown in the water of a river, an abundant and clear Polish river, like the Bug or the Vistula, or any kind of river. And these ashes also are mixed with tons of ashes coming from tons of other corpses, from tons of Jews. Burdensome. One can see that required "special measures." Well, by coincidence they called it simply "special handling"—*Sonderbehandlung*. Why look for complications where there are none? "Special handling" is simple and clear. And in the name of even greater simplicity they abbreviated it as *SB*. And those who carried out these very "special measures" were put into a special commando, a *Sonderkommando*. Which, in all their correspondence, they abbreviated as *SK*. And the *SK* were Jews. It was the Jews themselves who handled these "measures"; they were called, and saw themselves as, "dirty Jews."

Which is why Jewish death prompts him to remove his hat. Which is also ridiculous. And for two reasons. First, because in the presence of Jewish death it's customary to wear a hat, not remove it. Second, because Mathieu never wears a hat. At least not until recently. He borrowed Esther's cap. He asked his parents to lend it to him. What does he plan to do with it? He doesn't know. It was the summer of 1982.

Esther's Cap

Wearing this cap, Mathieu at first "plays at being Jewish." He wanders about, much as his sister used to do, in the streets, into stores, trying to gauge the impression he makes on people. Can they tell that he's Jewish? He catches the reflection of his face in store windows, in mirrors, and he sees in it a Jew. In any case, an SS man would have recognized him immediately. But there are no more SS. Perhaps Esther regretted it, that there are no more SS. No more SS to recognize Jews in the street, round them up, make them climb into trucks, tell them that they're being "relocated" to a better place, a place where they will be able to work, a place where their children will be able to go to school, and then gas them, then and there, right in those trucks, just like that, in the five minutes the ride takes—no need even to transport them to a place conceived for that purpose, bigger, more convenient, more efficient. Because at the time, places conceived for that purpose didn't yet exist. There were only trucks then, gas trailers. No, Esther couldn't have known that fate; for that, too, she was born too late. And besides, she was born in France, not in Poland. It's true that she could have been deported from Grenoble with Fanny, in 1943 or 1944. She even missed that by a hair. But as far as the gas trailers in Chelmno are concerned, or the SS trucks of the *Einsatzgruppen* in Poland, and in the Ukraine, no, that would not have been possible, sorry. Nor the Warsaw Ghetto. So many things that she couldn't have known. The ghetto she could only have imagined, read books, studied photographs—all so intensely that she succeeded in believing herself one of the fighters. Wearing a cap. And led to the *Umschlagplatz*, and brutally shoved into a wagon, very brutally. And setting out for the northeast. The Warsaw-Bialystok line with a stop midway. Treblinka they call this village. Pretty little train station. And flowers. Yes indeed, flowers. There's no doubt that we'll work here, and eat our fill. But why so much brutality to make us disembark? Maybe they're in a hurry. In a hurry to put us to work. And then the undressing, the shearing of hair, the path to heaven, why these brutalities? Receipt of soap, why these brutalities? And the lungs catching fire. The brutalities stopped. And so has life.

Walking in the streets wearing this cap, Mathieu looks people in the eye. He tries to meet their gaze. They, on the other hand, seem not to notice him. What blindness, what indifference! But the thing is, these people are not SS. They're people, simply people. Not only don't they detect a Jew in him, they don't even see him. It's like before, without the cap. He was a pure ghost, and pure ghost he remains. Commonplace. He's not threatened at all. He's not Esther after all.

Esther's great superiority, her incomparable superiority, lies in the fact that she'd been threatened. Born after the war, Mathieu can never catch up. Beat her on her own turf? She, who already had missed the "train." Who ate away at herself for having been neither victim nor fighter, cap or no cap, and for still being here, alive. It made her sick.

The truth is that he never loved Esther. He doesn't love her, period. All that he thinks, all that he imagines, all that he discovers, she had already thought, already imagined, already discovered. She'd completed the course a long time ago. She always walks ahead of him; it's unbearable. Today Mathieu writes in order to bear it. But even in this she precedes him, a shadow that he cannot overtake. He strives to follow it, to trample it. Trample her shadow. He's made up his mind: he'll have her die in Treblinka, he'll finally give her the death she wanted. With the others. But first he will bring her to life. That way, once and for all he'll trample the ever-present shadow of her corpse.

The first time Mathieu wore Esther's cap was at her burial in the Bagneux cemetery. Mathieu disguised himself for his sister. Since he had to cover his head, might as well be with her own cap, he told himself. Perhaps it gave her pleasure there, beyond the grave, to have close to her, on her death, this symbol of the ghetto, of a mythology that she alone could construe, a very secret and closed sect with its rituals, its cult objects, its ex–voto—the whole shebang devoted to death, the death she did not have!

Mathieu kept the cap. He wears it as he writes. Yes, he's writing. And she, was she writing? Is he then taking her place? Like the other Esther, Aunt Esther, who took Fanny's "place," in July 1942 in Paris when the police came to 27, rue des Couronnes, Paris 20? Took the place of the dead woman, the place of a woman whom "they" had decreed would die? Is the place of a dead person vacant so that anyone can occupy it? Or is it the opposite, is it that you mustn't touch it, just as Charles and Fanny had the fundamental decency to leave Esther's room intact? All in all, Mathieu is disgusted with himself. He's writing in disgust. A disgusting sewer, that's what he is.

Madame Supervisor

Each morning at the agency, at precisely nine o'clock as some employee presses the elevator button, people greet each other with the eternal joke: "Well, Madame Dumas, Monsieur Lautremond, going up to seventh heaven?" A rather worn-out joke no one can resist smiling at, if somewhat mechanically.

Mathieu Litvak's supervisor is Mme Roubestan. What's great about being boss, she likes to repeat, is that you are your own boss. Mathieu always agrees with her. What she doesn't realize, he thinks to himself, is that she herself has a boss, M. Sallustre.

Mme Roubestan is the same age as Esther. The age that Esther would have been if. Fortyish. Also the same long black hair that she pulls up into a pseudo-medieval bun that makes her look older. Esther used to wear her hair loose down her back; it reached to her hips and made her look like a young girl. Mathieu never dared make the slightest remark to Mme Roubestan about her hairdo; she's always known how to keep her distance. After all, she's the boss, isn't she? She would have been a perfect Kapo. Mathieu sometimes tells himself that. Then he's suspicious of her for a while. But not for long because he quickly realizes that his mind is wandering.

Esther's Hair

It's summer. Yanick has been sent to summer camp in the mountains. Esther and Mathieu are to go together to a camp in Brittany. She must be fourteen, and Mathieu nine. In those days she didn't eat. Well, she ate very little. She couldn't have weighed much. Her cheeks grew more and more hollow so that she began to look frightening. Fanny blamed this whim on the women's magazines her daughter reads, with their emphasis on dieting. She's wrong: these aren't at all her reasons. Coming home from the store one evening, and as if he just noticed how she looks, Charles asks her if she hasn't lost her mind. She looks like she just got out of Auschwitz! And all three stare at her with compassion. Esther runs out and slams the door to her room. She comes back a few minutes later, dressed like a concentration camp inmate, head shaved. Fanny faints, falls like a dead weight to the floor. Charles runs to her, talks to her, slaps her. Mathieu starts crying. The next day he catches sight of his mother in the hall; she holds, rolled up in one arm, the striped pajamas Esther got who knows where, and in her other hand, the hair razor.

Afterward no one ever mentioned the incident. Esther gave up her "diet." She even put on weight.

Her Death

That his sister was buried in a Jewish grave pleased Mathieu. He found that rather fitting. Well, pleased is not exactly the word. And in what other kind of grave could she have been interred? She hadn't bothered to leave any instruction, or any message. For someone who loved to write, it's, at the very least, inexplicable. She left without a flourish, with no comment. Which adds to their grief. Granted, she was "sick," but even so, why? They questioned Simon for a long time, and, after a while, talked at length to him about her. He was also at sea; he knew no more than they did. Mathieu suspected otherwise. Why then was he so overwhelmed, so much so that his in-laws had to convince him, over and over again, that she was "sick," and that it was incurable. It wasn't his fault, he must never think that. He was in no way to blame, neither were they, no one was. Except perhaps the war. . . . She was sick because of the past, a past she hadn't known, but that pursued her.

Simon often saw her writing. He knew that she wrote. He'd seen the sheets of paper pile up on her desk. But he'd never read any of her work. She had forbidden it. Besides, no one had ever read anything she wrote. That's what Simon said in those days. Later he told Mathieu that she had a filmmaker friend of hers, Jacques Lipshitz, read some of her things. Which shows that Simon lied, that some details bothered him. In any case, before she died she destroyed everything. Yes she'll remain an enigma, one it would be foolish to try to penetrate. Might as well question this Lydia Polack she consulted the year before her suicide. But what could she have told them, and to what purpose?

After her death, life went on as usual, on the surface. But only on the surface. Because underneath the surface it was better not to look too close. Of course, they didn't forget Esther. How could they forget? But they never spoke about her. At least not until the summer of 1982. Then Mathieu thought about her again. Her death, which took place seven years earlier, really struck him only then. He questioned his parents. Saw Simon again. And Uncle Avrum. He bought a fat notebook. He invented another life for his sister, and another death. Perhaps the life and death she had imagined for herself. The life and death she couldn't live without.

Why, then, did Charles, his father, leave Warsaw before the war? What was it like on Nowolipie Street? What did it look like? And the streetcars, the synagogues, and the Vistula, and the Saxon Gardens, and Leszno, and the Danzig Station? Esther had never set foot in Warsaw but she knew it by heart. She must have spent hours, days, studying its topography from current maps and old ones. If she had been let loose in that city, she would have managed. Without hesitation. Wouldn't have had to ask for directions. "Sick" as she was. When she was little, dogs were her passion. When she grew up, it was Poland. And the war. Sick.

Playing

Esther hates Yanick, God knows why. Sometimes she takes him in her arms, but it's as though she wanted to harm him, as though she were getting ready to suffocate him. The caresses she prodigiously bestows on him are strangely like bruises. Fanny quickly pulls him away. When the three of them are together, Esther loses patience immediately, becomes irritated, gets angry. She'll knock poor Yanick down and start hitting him. And knowing or thinking it's a game at first, Yanick breaks into laughter but soon bursts into tears, runs and complains to Fanny who takes him up in her lap and strokes his chubby cheeks.

When their parents are out for the evening, and Yanick's asleep, Mathieu sometimes goes to his sister's room. She'll tolerate him but they don't speak: for Esther, Mathieu is invisible; he doesn't exist. He'll stand in front of the photograph above her bed, and each time ask her who are these women dressed up as men. She doesn't answer him. Here she is, sitting at her desk, studying. As usual. She always studies twice as much, first the material for her own grade, and then for the grade above that. Mathieu finally realized it. He doesn't ask her questions, especially not. It would be terrible. He's afraid to. He keeps quiet, makes no sound, only too happy to be admitted to this lair. Like a sensible person who wouldn't dream of disturbing the ceremonies of a strange cult he understands nothing about but is impressed by, he doesn't dare to disturb her. He no longer questions her about the large cap she's wearing. Doesn't dare. Sometimes he lies down on her bed and stares at the photograph on the wall. From time to time Esther needs to take a rest. She'll sit down near her brother for a moment, not saying a thing. He doesn't exist, really does not. The invisible man. He believes that he really is invisible. Esther could undress right there, in front of his eyes, without noticing that he's there. He expects her to do it. He hopes that she will, and that he'll see her. That she has never done it leads him to believe that perhaps he's not totally invisible. His eyes don't leave the photograph. There lies his sister's secret—a secret exposed to all eyes, therefore even more of a secret. A secret so plain and obvious that he says to himself, no, that can't be her secret, or it's a secret that conceals yet another one that only she knows. The secret of a secret. Sitting on the edge of her bed, Esther looks toward the window, gazing vaguely at a vague sky. What is she thinking of? Why doesn't she say anything? Mathieu doesn't dare to speak. He doesn't know what he's afraid of.

Once he was overcome by a sort of madness. He must have been six or seven. Something like a need for tenderness. He turned toward her, and saying her name, put his arms around her neck. She leaned over him, and the dark rain of her hair blinded him. He put a hand on her breast and asked her if she had milk. She didn't answer. Or perhaps he was dreaming? That's it, he must have dreamed it; it's inconceivable otherwise.

But these screams, these sudden howls? It's probably Yanick who woke up from a nightmare. He got up and came to join them in his big sister's room. When he sees them he stops crying. He's stupefied: it must be a bewitching scene, Esther leaning over Mathieu. They stare at him silently. Yanick's eyes are haloed by pretty, blue circles; his blond, angelic curls are all tangled. Once past his surprise he's joyful at their "coupling." He yells triumphantly, straddles an invisible but noisy and glorious mare, invisible but luminous, invisible but winged in silver, in red and yellow flames. And the angel draws a circle of fire around the room and runs off. Yes, Mathieu must have dreamed it.

The Past, Again

Mathieu called his mother. Would she tell him about those days, the war, Esther's birth? But she's already told him about all that. It's not very clear, could she tell him again, if it's not too painful for her? Painful? No, not at all, why should it be painful for her? It's not as if she had been. . . . No, after all, she came back with Esther! She wasn't . . . well, he knows, he knows what she means . . . No, he doesn't. Yes, he knows.

Hierarchy

Mme Roubestan informed Mathieu that he's been promoted. She had him sign a paper, and gave him a copy. He's going to get a pay raise. With perhaps a rather important retroactive increment. Mathieu telephoned his parents right away; they were overjoyed. Oh, no need to exaggerate. It's not like getting your doctorate. No, but, still, it's not a trifle either!

Now that Esther is dead, it's easy for Mathieu to shine in his parents' eyes. While his sister was alive it would have been a waste of time. With the exception of the birth of his son, Julien. There I had Esther beat. How could she have competed with that—with life? Even with twenty-five doctorates!

Yes, Esther is dead. But her younger brother has been climbing his way up, hasn't he? Slowly but incontestably he's advancing. He's moved up two notches since her death. How quickly time passes. . . . The last was the same time that Esther disappeared, in 1975. A sign from heaven, in some way. Who knows, maybe Esther would have been happy to learn the good news. Maybe she wouldn't have. . . . Or would have waited a few hours, a few days? Could have won that. She could have held out another week. Who knows? A week is nothing to sneeze at. Just think, being alive for seven more days.

7

Sometimes, when he happens to be at work a little early or a little late, he'll be the only one by the elevator. He'll press the call button and wait. While he's waiting for the elevator, God, yes, God himself joins him in the game. A tightly matched game. A game played in seven innings, seven seconds, seven twinklings of time in which his lot and God's disposition toward him are decided right then and there. Nothing less. The game consists in timing the arrival of the elevator with the count of seven. The number 7? Yes. Mathieu will count to seven in his head, pressing his thumb and index finger together seven times, imperceptibly (but not, of course, to God). Sometimes he cheats a little by drawing out his counting, waiting slightly longer than necessary between one and seven. Or, if the elevator is faster than predicted, he'll do just the opposite—accelerate and count faster. It's as though his life were at stake. If the elevator and the number seven come at the same time, God is with him. If not, God abandons him. And why? Because one day while leafing through one of Mathieu's French books, Esther fell upon a poem by Victor Hugo from *Les Châtiments* that told of the taking of Jericho by the Israelites. She was probably familiar with the poem, but it was as if she discovered it for the first time. Holding the book in her hand, she began to read it in a slow, inspired way, going round and round the room like the Israelites circling Jericho. Mathieu could feel her going round and round behind his back, and it bothered him. He felt like escaping but didn't dare; his sister was supposed to be giving him private lessons. When she finished reciting the poem (Mathieu hadn't really been listening and hadn't retained much of the poem because he was fuming inside), Esther took the trouble to explain, or to convince herself of the beauty of the text, its depth, or so it seemed to him. She then treated him to a series of somewhat demented exclamations. The toppling of the walls of Jericho! On the seventh round! On the seventh day! When the trumpets of the people led by Joshua blew for the seventh time! Seven! Seven! Seven! Yes, that was the number. You get it, Mathieu? Seven! Seven! The number . . . But Mathieu didn't get it at all. And when, after calming down, she asked him once again if he got the picture, and rather than lying he said no, that he didn't get it, what was there to get? She rewarded him by hitting him on the head and calling him an ass. He grabbed her arm then and bit her fiercely. Since that day the number 7 had remained something of a symbol for Mathieu. Not really a symbol. An obsession rather. Actually he had no idea what it could be a symbol of. He never spoke about it to anyone. Besides, he only thinks about it when he's waiting alone for the elevator at work. If there's a colleague with him he never thinks of God, the number 7, Jericho, Joshua, the walls, the trumpets. Esther probably would have been interested in all this. Perhaps she would have found her brother less boring. He would have become worthy in her eyes. They might have been able to speak, after all. Even though Mathieu was not born during the war and hadn't been threatened.

Thirty-two Years

Mathieu didn't know those days. For him, it's as if they never existed. What can he do about it? Nothing. Therefore he wishes they had never existed. Sometimes he says, these years did not exist. Yes, there was the war, a war, but a war like all the others, like World War I, with its death and slaughter. Like the other wars. Nothing more, nothing less. Like all the others. Charles's parents, and Fanny's mother and sister, died during that war like all the others, or even because of the war like the others. A stray bullet, a bomb fragment. Even better—real sickness, cholera, typhus. And Charles, he was a soldier like any other. He killed Germans just as the Germans killed Frenchmen, Poles. This was war, what can you expect! With its trenches, Maginot lines, Atlantic walls, battles, Midways, Pearl Harbors, Oradour-sur-Glanes, even Hiroshimas. A war like any other. Worse than the others, granted, because of progress, which can't be stopped. But that women and children were deported was absurd. Totally useless. Women, children, and old people are always killed in wars. They're killed by chance. Bombs fall blindly, and it happens that women, children, and old people are in the way. By chance. The intent was to kill, of course, but not necessarily this or that woman or child. It's a matter of chance, luck. Bad luck. You happen to be standing in the way of a bomb, or nearby, and, unfortunately, you are killed. By luck, bad luck. But that they deport women, children, and old people in order to kill them, that precisely those women, children, and old people are to die not by chance, or accident, or luck, but by design, is absurd, illogical, makes no sense at all. It didn't happen. It didn't happen because it could not have happened. Esther is making it up. She's a mental case. Everyone knows that she's sick. Deported, her? Yes, since she says so. Born in Warsaw, Esther? She says so. Mathieu is totally lost. Who could make something of that story? What tsetse fly bit her that she's decked out in the mask of sleep? At dinner, with Yanick, they make fun of her absent gaze; wake up, Esther, we've arrived, everyone out . . . They hit the nail on the head. We have arrived, where? Get out of what train? The train that goes from Warsaw to Bialystok, with a stop at Treblinka, pretty village, end of the line. But what about Esther, who's smiling, like a pretty half-wit? Sometimes they feel like grabbing her and shaking her. They don't dare. They're too afraid of the cutting, scornful words that she'd heap on them. The only one she respects is Charles, whom she insists on calling Adek. He was born in Warsaw. He was in the Resistance. Oh, please, tell me about that again, tell me about the militia, the Gestapo, and Warsaw. What was it like? And the Vistula River, frozen in winter, where you could swim in the summer, and Mylna, and Nalewki, and Nowolipie, and Bonifraterska, and Nowolipie, and Ptachia, and why there were herring on Ptachia. Enough! The others, Fanny, Mathieu, Yanick, don't want to hear the stories about those bygone days, don't want to hear the names of those strange streets picked off once more; they have no desire to learn them. That doesn't concern them. It's over and done with. Those days are dead and gone. But for Esther they're not dead and gone. Or, they're dead and gone but not buried. Because it's not enough for those things to be dead and gone, not at all. They still have to be buried. And for Esther, they simply were not buried. Not for Esther, nor for anyone else, for that matter. Which is why, not being buried, those days come back to haunt us. For example, during the war in Lebanon, in the summer of 1982. That's the reason you could read and hear that *Israel* = SS. For that very reason. For no other. Because those days are gone but not buried.

Charles said that life stopped for him when his daughter died. In truth, it had stopped way before then. Life had stopped the day after the Liberation when he learned that, in the Warsaw Ghetto, his mother, Raisl, had given herself up to the Germans. And when Esther, his daughter, died, turning herself over to death the way his mother had to the Germans, then Charles knew, perhaps, that his mother was really dead. It took all that time, thirty-two years, thirty-two years during which Charles's life left no trace on anything, during which he nurtured with delight the revulsion, the horror of the event. Because for him the only momentous event would have been the news that his mother had not died, that a miracle had occurred, that he'd been misinformed. All the rest, what he heard on the radio, these distant rumors of battles, of sedition, of coups d'état, of repression, all the rest—faint stirrings on the surface of the planet. And when his wife asked him now and then, "It's good for us?," he wouldn't even bother to answer.

A Number

What's that, the inscription on Esther's arm? A numeral, a number. What number? According to his sister, Mathieu is too young to understand. But he persists. It's a number, she says, that was tattooed on the arms of the deportees when they arrived in the camp. At least, on the arms of those who weren't gassed immediately. What deportees? What camp? Was she herself deported? Yes, she was. To Treblinka, in Poland. She brings her arm up to her mouth and bites deeply into her flesh.

"Look," she says, "see this bite? That's what an SS dog did to me. His name was Bari, a German Shepherd, that's what he was called. One of their dogs, their very cruel dogs, who used to bite the deportees when they arrived."

"But were you born in Warsaw or in France?" Mathieu asks. "I don't really understand."

"In Warsaw, on Mylna Street. Look, that's me in the picture. And that cap I'm wearing there, look, I still have it."

"It's not possible!"
Let him ask Momma, he'll see!

Silence

Maybe Mathieu will manage to write the book that Esther was to write and that no one has read. Because he's writing, isn't he? That's what he's doing now, isn't it? Esther will never know about it, thank God. She wouldn't have allowed it. She would have asked him why he was butting in, what business was it of his, and Mathieu would have been speechless at that question, acquiescing—indeed, indeed, what business was it of his, acquiescing, admitting, acknowledging his guilt—he was guilty of giving up his rightful place, of having usurped another's place, another's role. Only survivors had a right to speak. The others, especially those born after the war, should keep quiet, be silent. Their words are obscene, impudent. That's what Esther would have said. But what about her? Even though Esther was born during the war, what did she know actually? What had she experienced that Mathieu had not? What had she witnessed still in the cradle? Yes, she had escaped the train and Drancy. But she had escaped it, which is the point. She and Fanny had escaped the convoy to the East. As for the rest, she had been told. Or she had read it. Or she had imagined it. Just like Mathieu, nothing more. What right does she have to talk about Warsaw? What has she to say that she actually experienced herself? Treblinka? Auschwitz? But even her parents are alive. *Nothing* happened to them. Nothing. Yes, Fanny saw the disappearance of her mother and sister, Rivka and Esther. Yes, Charles lost his mother, his sister, one of his brothers—Raisl, Guta, Bolek. But Esther? What suffering and what bereavement?

Only the Written Words Will Remain

Even though she claims otherwise, Esther is not writing. At dinner, when they're all together, they fight about it. Esther gets up on her high horse, flies into a rage, leaves the room, slamming the door as usual. Nobody pays any attention, and in her absence the meal livens up. Simon runs after her, and screams can be heard coming from Esther's room. Simon returns to the dining room. Something is wrong with her.

"Poor Simon," says Fanny. "How can you bear . . ."

They quickly change the subject and speak of trips, the purchase of an apartment, a new shop, of the agency, the Faculty of Sciences, of Julien . . . How to talk about everyday happenings with Esther? Mathieu has nothing in common with her, except, perhaps, memories of childhood. And, besides, are they even referring to the same childhood? Esther admits to preserving a horrifying remembrance of the past, an unbearable feeling of loneliness, of ennui, of grayness. What inspired these misconceptions? Mathieu and Yanick never tire of recalling a childhood that was full of laughs, of games, of shared secrets.

Ghostly Esther, with her pale cheeks and dark eyes and her cap. And her jealousy.

When Mathieu's son, Julien, was born, Esther didn't bother to visit. Which surprised no one. Her absence in the hospital went unnoticed. Granted, she called a week later. Mathieu was dying to ask her stop by and visit, but he held back. He was too afraid of an evasive response: she was very busy these days, she would try her best. In truth, she had lots of time, a huge amount, since she no longer was teaching, she was idle, intent on the total freedom which she needed, she claimed, to write her book. What book? And Mathieu, talking to her on the telephone, said nothing, listening to her half amused, half furious, as she insincerely asked the usual questions, about the baby, about Véronique. As if she cared! Especially about Véronique, whom she despised, whom she had never accepted. Véronique was not Jewish. This was the great sin, the quasi-sacrilege: to marry a *goye*. To marry a *goye* after Hitler, she said, was to advance his project, to complete his work. She gassed herself a few weeks later. Perhaps because of this birth. She could see that life went on. That life did not stop in 1943. In fact, who was it that carried on the Nazi enterprise, Mathieu who married a *goye* and gave life, or Esther who married a Jew but walled herself in a ghetto destroyed in 1943? For example, what horrified her most of all was that Poland should still exist. That a country which was nothing but an archipelago of charnel houses should still exist. That people should still exist there. That life would again flourish there, that trees could dare to grow again from the ashes of corpses—all was for her a scandal, ultimate proof that God did not exist. To her, Poland was a woman appallingly raped, and the Jews of Poland the womb that was violated, ravaged, torn. For Esther, the Jews of Poland were the womb of Poland. A. H. had wanted to turn this land into a sterile woman. He had fastened on her womb. He had injected it with gallons and gallons of Zyklon B. And, in spite of everything, life reappeared, an obscene life. Esther had indeed needed to consult this Lydia Polack, someone with precisely that ironic name. She couldn't have done better. Even though they were separated, she told Simon everything about the conversa-

tions she and Lydia had months before her suicide. For
Mathieu, it was something of a mystery that his sister had
chosen Simon Pessakowicz. Not that he questioned his
intelligence: he was reputed to be a renowned scientific
researcher. But he wasn't refined, not at all literary,
rather a bon vivant, fond of bad puns, a big drinker of
wine who frequented restaurants catering to a wealthy,
vulgar clientele. . . . The exact opposite of Esther, or so
it seemed. So what happened? All in all, the only explanation Mathieu could find for his sister choosing such a
companion was that Simon's parents had been deported.
And had not come back. Esther could grant everything
to such an orphan. He was the only one she would confide
in. He alone was worthy of her. Equipped with such dep-
rivations, such prestige.

Mathieu telephoned Simon. No, he had no objection
to speaking about Esther. He didn't ask about the reasons for this curiosity, a delayed curiosity. He even
thought his curiosity normal. Yet Mathieu hesitated.
Something was bothering him, something he couldn't
quite put his finger on. Did it have to do with Esther?
With Simon Pessakowicz? Or simply with the truth?
That's it—to learn the truth perhaps? Or did it have to
do with this process, this questioning, rummaging around
in matters that didn't concern him, that were not his own.
Perhaps it showed a lack of sensitivity. Granted, he didn't
love Esther much. But in spite of everything, she represented someone very close to him, and not only because
she was his sister. Someone who was older than him, and
who, simply because of the date of her birth, could have
straightaway died in a gas chamber. She was contemporary with this pure and simple possibility, that people
could die in gas chambers, herself included. The moment
of her birth coincided, to the very minute, with the gas-

sing of thousands of people. She was a contemporary of that. Simply because of the date of her birth. Like Simon. Which is why Mathieu *had* to hear Simon. And hear Fanny again. And Charles. And Uncle Avrum, old Uncle Avrum. Before time ran out and there would be no one left, no one in the world who had been a contemporary. Then it would be the end. The voice of those people would be gone. There would be nothing more than written words, skimpy and ridiculous written words. Nothing.

He felt that he couldn't stop up his ears forever, pretending that he knew. He knew nothing. Had never wanted to know. Esther, she'd wanted to know so much that she had exposed herself, and was burned by the mortal flame of that knowledge. She had ended up joining the dead. But what more was there to know that Mathieu didn't know already? What did this knowledge consist of? Dates, numbers? To put yourself in the shoes of those who died? To look at death as they had, and to feel it slip into you the way they had felt it slip into them, into their throats, their bronchial tubes? To become that porous? To catch up with the rolling train, the missed train that had carried them over there, to *Pitchipoi?* Impossible! You had to turn your back on this train. Leave the station. Not hang around, not look back. Don't look back on Sodom-Auschwitz or, like Orpheus, on Eurydice. And yet, this mystery. This inscrutable mystery, like the number 7 for Mathieu. An empty symbol. An obsession. Or an enigma he could turn round in his mind, circle it seven times, yet the walls would not give way. Where did this feeling of shame come from? What was so intangible and shameful? Why this prohibition? Because Mathieu hadn't yet been born when *that* was going on? It wasn't even a question of escape. Luck had nothing to do with it: he hadn't been born yet! There was the sin and the forced silence. His shame was the very reason he now needed the figure of his sister. Through Esther he mapped out his shame, embodied his guilt. He named it: Esther Litvak. Thanks to this name he could at last write, even in disgust, in self-disgust, and not only about himself but about the whole thing. In truth, it wasn't a desire for knowledge that animated him. Because he knew, he knew everything. But he simply had to write about that knowledge, get it down in black and white. To get past the disgust.

The Play

No waves, no hitches. Any hitch is a misfortune. Any thought of change gives him nightmares. Like the news of his promotion at the agency; Véronique couldn't understand how it affected her husband. When they spoke of it, Mathieu realized that the wish to keep his place, preferably the most insignificant place, was for him a matter of atonement. For what crime did he have to atone? He didn't know. What did he have to conceal, to mask, to erase? What secret lay unconscious in him that, with the least modification in his life, would surface like a corpse—a corpse that a murderer had been tempted to drown in a lake. It was his special fate to play a bit part in a play he hadn't written, a play performed years before his birth, with its own actors and audience. And once the curtain was down, he had to remain on stage with the others, like him, born after the performance, or during, or before, remembering the play they had seen or acted in, as torturer or as victim. Was he waiting for the curtain to go up again?

Far from Shore

Esther was not writing. Those last days, having given up teaching, she would have spent stretched out on her unmade bed, eyes to the ceiling. Inspiration is slow to come, well, let's sleep, kiddo, wrest a few hours from this long life, so long and useless. When will it all end? When will I have the victory that frees me at last from life, from waiting?

Simon and Esther separated, perhaps temporarily, perhaps not, in the fall of 1974. That summer she had gone to New York. When she returned, they stopped living together. She didn't go back to work at the *lycée*. Mathieu imagines her starting to drift far from shore, holed up and disoriented. No one noticed. Except Simon perhaps. Motionless, abandoned by everything, she slipped imperceptibly into a frozen world of unreality, with its nightmares of dogs.

The few words that pass between Mathieu and his sister—bubbles that burst as soon as they're formed. In the end, she's only interested in herself. As for the others, they're all mediocre, aren't they? So pedestrian, so dense.

At the Litvaks, she's the only one who really matters. Mathieu and Yanick could disappear under the table. They can no longer breathe.

Who will remember this black sheep? Maybe a dozen teenagers? Mme Litvak? Oh yes, Mme Litvak, that petite brunette with her wild hair, who used to bug us with Racine's tragedy *Esther*? Of course we remember. (She preferred to keep her maiden name, rather more sparse, that's true, than Pessakowicz.) Only Simon could have known what went on in her head, in her life, those last days before her act. But they no longer saw each other.

Toba's Memories

Mathieu made himself go to see Uncle Avrum. He wanted him to talk about the Warsaw Ghetto where the

125

Germans had sent him, and the others, after its liquidation. In truth, he simply wanted to listen to him. To hear him, to be able to hear, for the first time in his life, someone tell about *that*. He questioned him about the Ghetto. So that he wouldn't have to say to him: tell me about *that*. That was a request Mathieu could not have put into words. Even though his uncle, the brother of his grandfather Szymon Tenenbaum, had already consented. But the Warsaw Ghetto, Uncle Avrum didn't remember it too well. He had only been there a month when he was sent back to his own camp in Silesia. On the other hand, his wife, Toba, remembered very well. So well and so clearly that one would think that she herself had lived through those things when, in reality, she was in Paris during the war, waiting for Avrum, and trying not to get deported herself. What she is most intent on recounting is the *Totenmarsch*. That's how she says it, in German. It's so nice in German. In French too, *marche de la mort*, death march. Brings to mind a line of boy scouts, cub scouts, lighthearted, bucolic, on their way to an amusement park. So while Avrum talks and tries to organize his memories, when he's silent and hesitates, she urges him to get to the *Totenmarsch*, not to forget it. That's what interests her, what seems important. That's what she remembers best, that's what made her suffer the most, she says. Avrum must have told her so often about this march.

A Dybbuk

Once again Mathieu went to see Simon, his brother-in-law. Simon spoke of Esther and himself, of the two of them as a couple, of their separation. At times he seemed to speak freely, almost detached, evoking Esther not so much as a dead person but as dead, above all, to him; other times, there were reticences, averted glances, hesitations, vagueness. Mathieu felt that talking was difficult for Simon, that he was ashamed perhaps to open up in this way, to betray the love he had felt for Esther or that he still felt, that in speaking about her as if behind her back (but what other way could you speak about her from now on if not behind her back?) he were insulting her beyond the grave. Or, perhaps, rather than shame, what he felt was guilt, for having contributed even in some small way to her death. On the other hand, Mathieu sensed that he had a need to speak, a need to unload, get rid of a weight, a burden of memories that in fact took the place of another burden, just as difficult to unload, a more distant event, yet still raw, brute, and brutal— the deportation in 1942 of his parents from Paris. Fearing the worst, they had been cautious enough to entrust their child to some relatives in the suburbs, just a few days before their own arrest. But Simon could never get rid of that burden—his parents' deportation, or his wife's suicide—simply by recounting his memories; it never made him feel lighter. Because, in reality, no burden is unloaded by talking; talking doesn't get rid of anything. The speaker doesn't become lighter by talking; on the contrary, he takes on yet an additional burden, the burden of shame. The shame of speaking. Because he's prey to a strange haunting, a blockage, something foreign in him, an automaton leading its own life, sleeping and waking at will, a dybbuk inside, separate, over which he has no control, even if he thinks he can talk about it, pretend to describe its appearance, imagine himself laughing about it. And this strange, unfamiliar voice, which is his voice yet not his voice, is the voice of the dybbuk in him, with whom he is joined yet entirely distinct: Simon imagines he's guilty of *having sent his parents to their death so that he himself could be spared.* It may be that this guilt that Mathieu attributes disparagingly to Simon is nothing but the murky shadow of his own unconscious guilt. Little by little he allowed the reality of his sister's suicide, finally acknowledged, to penetrate, and it was, for him, a replica in miniature of what the Jewish people had experienced forty years earlier. To dare speak of either event constituted the worst of indecencies. He would write in shame the book of shame, the very book Esther could not, would not manage to complete, to which she had preferred a definitive silence.

In Front of the Mirror

He just noticed that he'd misplaced Esther's cap. He'd have to find it. After all, it fit him well. Of course, he wouldn't have dreamed of wearing it at the agency. They would have looked at him funny. He wouldn't have dared. He sees his sister again in front of her mirror, imitating the pose of those young women in the photograph, regretting that she hadn't been with them in their struggle and misery. All she could do was to ape them, pitiful, alone in front of her mirror, taking advantage of the situation to inspect her unblemished skin, her pale complexion, to notice the budding wrinkles, the skin's grainy texture like that of an older woman. She tries on sad smiles: "I'm getting old, I am getting old. Already thirty-two and still nothing, nothing. My breasts sag, my shoulders and legs are creasing. I don't laugh anymore. I don't cry anymore. I don't listen anymore. I'm tired . . . I'll never have children, never. My little doll . . ." Words swallowed today in the black hole of the past. *Danse macabre.* Damp caves, mold of forgotten caves, ghetto sewers torched by

the flamethrowers, full of the decomposing corpses that
Uncle Avrum will discover at the end of 1943. Death
everywhere. Necrology. Kaddish.

The German Shepherd Bari

M. Sallustre, his boss's boss, summoned Mathieu to
notify him officially of his promotion. That day he had
him come to his office on the second floor, Room 212. He
immediately asked him to sit down on the fake-leather
armchair facing him and, as in the movies, offered him
a huge cigar, man to man, which, without knowing why,
Mathieu declined. There were posters of castles in Bavaria on the wall, behind M. Sallustre's desk. M. Sallustre was a fan of Wagner. Everybody at the office knew
about it. They say that he knew the *Ring* cycle by heart,
and went to Germany whenever he could for large help-
ings. When he returned, whether enchanted or disappointed, he would share his impressions with whomever
he could get to listen out of politeness or interest. He
was probably fond of beauties such as *Nacht und Nebel*,
niemand gleich. Night and Fog, Nuit et Brouillard,
Nacht und Nebel. Wagner. No Shakespeare, no Dante,
no Victor Hugo. Wagner!
Mathieu noticed on M. Sallustre's desk the framed
photograph of a German Shepherd. He asked if it was his
dog. Yes it was, his name was Bari, like Bari the German
Shepherd in the fine novel by Curwood that he was crazy
about as a child. No, Mathieu had never read it, at least
not that he remembered. He thought that his sister had
read it. He thought so.
Mathieu hated this man. He hated him immediately,
just like that. Or perhaps because of Wagner, of Germany, the castles in Bavaria, but mostly because of Bari.

Simon had told him that Esther was afraid of dogs, big dogs, especially German Shepherds. According to Simon, even Esther couldn't account for this phobia. Especially when she remembered that she'd been crazy about these same dogs as a child. Mathieu couldn't remember, perhaps he'd been too young. It had been a sentimental passion, said Simon, but a powerful one. When she was nine or ten, it seemed she knew countless breeds of dogs, maybe all of them. Her interest in breeds of dogs carried over, rather early on, to a passion for classifying races of people. She sought to find out where she belonged on the racial map. When asked about it, Fanny confirmed Simon's remarks. Esther read children's books about dogs, kept notebooks on them, wrote stories in which dogs were the heroes . . . Yet there had never been a dog in the house. For a whole year, Fanny said, she spoke of the German Shepherd Bari, the dog in a novel by Curwood.

Prehistory

Mathieu did not love Esther. He knew nothing about her. Or very little. He didn't know her. Something in her, or in him, prevented him from knowing or wanting to know her. Perhaps because she was older than him. Or perhaps the fact that she was born during the war made him cast her on his parents' side and on the side of their generation. On the prehistoric side. It wasn't only because this period had preceded him, but also because it had been a period unique in all of human history—a period when a state had wanted to annihilate an entire people from the face of the earth. Not out of malice, not because it was at war with it, not because this people represented a threat or a danger in its eyes. Not because it thwarted its plans, or opposed them in any way (because the German Jews would have been Nazis just like the other Germans had the Nazis not been anti-Semites), not because this people was so different from them or that it did not share their values. But because of mysterious, incomprehensible reasons. And just as mysteriously, just as incomprehensibly, Mathieu drew a feeling of shame from this very absence of reasons for the decreed extermination of the Jews during this period preceding his birth, the period in which Esther had first seen the light of day, but a day enclosed in a night such as humanity had never known. He didn't want to hear about it anymore. And he understood later, during the summer of 1982, that the disgust his sister provoked in him was due, and due only, to the period of her birth. But why this feeling of shame? Was it because the Jews themselves had masterminded their own extermination? Have yourself registered as Jews, they were told. And they eagerly inscribed themselves on lists, had the Jewish mark stamped on their identity papers. Wear the yellow star! And they sew it on. Or else, as in Poland, move into the "Jewish quarter." And they tell themselves, "there we will be safe." Someone comes to deport them? And they calmly pack their suitcases and obediently follow the militia or police. In the ghettos Jews compiled the list of names to meet the deportation quota, then organized the convoys. The Jewish police pushed Jews into the wagons. In the camps Jews undressed Jews, Jews shaved Jews, Jews shoved Jews into gas chambers after having given them a towel and some soap for the "shower"; Jews removed the corpses from the gas chambers; Jews buried, then unburied, the corpses, then burned them after extracting their gold teeth; and Jews made bundles of their clothes, bundles of shoes, bundles of eyeglasses, bundles of hair.

The machine seemed to work on its own. A few Ukrainian guards, a few SS oversaw the machine. You could almost do without them. And they themselves were surprised to see how well the machine worked on its own, how efficiently. That's what Franz Stangl, the commander of Treblinka, would later confide to a woman journalist. He was in Brazil after the war. One day as he was traveling, the train stopped next to a slaughterhouse. The cattle were parked in a pen and, from behind the gate, looked straight at Stangl. It made him feel ill at ease, this old SS man, being stared at like that by the cows. It reminded him of Poland, he said. This was how people had looked at him, trustingly, just before going into the boxes, as he called them. And it even took away his appetite. And he swore, this old SS man, that from now on he would never eat canned food.

The Secret

Mathieu does his utmost to prolong the last breath of a dead woman. But more and more he has the feeling of speaking in her place and, like a poor ventriloquist, being the only one who's speaking. This is the way, he thinks, to keep himself alive. So he speaks of a dead woman to let himself know that he exists, that he is alive. And, then, it's obvious that Esther Litvak is important only because she's dead. Alive, there would have been nothing to say about her. The living are prey to banality, that is, to evaluation, comparison. Only the dead escape that fate. They are immeasurable. The living are banal because they can be questioned, and the so-called mystery surrounding them penetrated, revealed for what it is—a false mystery, a banality. The dead escape banality because they cannot be questioned. They carry their secrets to the grave, as they say. Even if they have no secrets. Even if their secret is precisely that they have none. It's still a secret. The secret of banality. Maybe that's why someone commits suicide, to pretend she has a secret. One dies to disturb others. When a person dies an ordinary death, others don't care; they adjust to it sooner or later. All this changes if death is voluntary. Thus, death by deportation, for those who remain, is like suicide. A person dies before her time and with her secret intact. To love someone is perhaps to want to wrest away her secret. That's what is meant by the desire to possess. Suicide, death by deportation, allows a person to escape being possessed. Then the others, those who remain, are angry at themselves for not having had the time, for not having taken the time, to extract the dead person's secret. For not having loved her enough. And they tell themselves that the person died because of that. And that it's their fault. Because they weren't able to love. And, yet, Auschwitz is more cruel than suicide. For in some way the deported person attests by his departure to his absolute love for those who were spared. Someone is always deported in place of someone else. Even if, most of the time, it's nothing more than a question of luck, bad luck. In the Warsaw Ghetto, to escape a roundup was to believe that you still had a chance to survive. And the more time passed, the more you knew for certain, even though you wouldn't hear of it, that the people who were taken, and bound for God-knows-where, had given you that extra chance to survive. They were dying in your place.

Two or Three Things He Knows about Her

She likes to be noticed. On social occasions, she wouldn't consent, for anything in the world, to sit on the sidelines. She has to be at the center of things. If, by chance, someone else should be the center of the gathering, she'd sneak away, run it down to anyone who would listen. She's always trying to bowl people over; and it often happens that this ambition will backfire. Then she finds herself humiliated. It seems that only proud people are susceptible to such mortal vexations. It leaves them with a lasting desire for revenge—although they don't know who or what they're avenging—a thirst that's quenched only with their death. . . . She was always very ambitious. . . . She would come home sad even when she took first place in math, or received a very high grade in composition.

"Why should that make me so happy?" she would wonder. "I'm first only in a group of dunces. If it's me—so mediocre, so beneath it all, so wretched a student, a zero—who's always in first place, it must mean that something is wrong, that I'm not in the right place, that I'll never be in the right place anywhere . . ."

There, even in her success at school, she saw an irrefutable sign of being cursed, of exclusion, of disgrace—yet more tangible proof of her solitude. And what unseemly joy when she took only second place! At last she's "normal," no longer distinguished. And yet she has a constant need to distinguish herself. Mathieu doesn't understand it at all.

The Necrophore

What an idiot! Mathieu just found his cap. Would you believe it? It was on his head. He ran to look at himself in the mirror, to judge the effect. Not bad . . . Sitting at his desk, tracing these words, he thinks of himself as one of the Talmudic scribes among his ancestors, insofar as there was one among them, which is doubtful. He likes to wear a hat while he writes. Because he's really in the process of writing, isn't he? (Esther must be turning over in her grave!)

Sometimes he thinks that Esther is only the fruit of his imagination. That she never existed except inside himself. Like a part of himself. A dead part. An empty zone. Therefore, by writing, by trampling his sister's corpse, isn't he simply strutting on this empty stage? If it weren't for that palpable figure, he thinks, he would be a cannibal. This is how it works: Mathieu imagines that something in him, which he calls Esther, is dead. His murky desire to kill this thing mingles with the very desire to write *about* the death, sleep with it, making of this rottenness his nourishment—a twofold, antithetical yet identical, desire for life and death. It's like the necrophore, an insect that lays its eggs inside the cadaver of another animal, which its larvae later feed on. In some ways, Mathieu's words dance on the decaying belly of his sister, on her breasts and her neck and her thighs. There's no doubt that he's writing in her place. He's stealing from her. He's stealing her book. Since it's said that you *carry* a book inside yourself, then Mathieu must be foraging in Esther's gut, laying his eggs on her entrails. He's stealing her death, he's stealing her life. Sometimes he feels that the words he puts down on paper are digging his own grave. And he wonders if Esther really was writing. Basically he knows nothing about her. Nothing. He uses her name, that's all, her name and two or three probable, possible, or likely things about her. Is that a major crime?

The name Esther Litvak, like each milligram of ash from Auschwitz, is scattered, for Mathieu, like so many invisible sparks in the night of the world, which is the night the writer writes in. Darkness of absence and unreality. The writer's words redeem nothing, remain powerless to retrieve the exiled sparks.

The Eye Was in the Grave

Under the dark gaze of the rabbi, Mathieu, like the others, threw a spade of earth on Esther's coffin. He felt almost dizzy standing above the gaping pit. The next few nights he dreamed that he had slipped into that pit, and that the earth closed forever on top of him. On both of them. Serves me right, he told himself, I earned it. Every crime demands punishment. But what crime? At the cemetery he felt Uncle Avrum's insistent glance focused on him. He seemed to reproach him for something. For a minute he thought of talking to him. But he didn't dare.

Scenarios

Esther's power. Her imagination. Her taste for violence and cruelty. She made up scenarios and dragged Mathieu along. Sometimes she took the role of "the prisoner"—a game she invented—and she would mime a dead or fainting woman. Straddling her, Mathieu had to participate in the brutal game. Which of the two gained the most pleasure, Mathieu in touching her or Esther in being caressed and bruised?

An Ogress

She was capable of laughter, Esther was. The laughter of an ogress in an instant turning into a flood of tears. An ogress capsizing like a barrel, and each time it made Mathieu uneasy. One never would have guessed her so unhappy under her hilarious exterior, yes, often hilarious. She hid her game well. Or rather, she wasn't playing. She was made for happiness, and something—but what?—kept her from it. A small thing, a gear that needed oiling. It wouldn't have taken much for it to work.

2

Number 27, rue des Couronnes, was the corner house
at the intersection of rue Bisson. At that time there was
a handsome café on the ground floor of the building,
handsome compared to the dilapidated building itself, or
to the street, which was a street of poor people. Yet, after
the war, it took "them" a long time to demolish it all:
the café, the building, the entire street along with the
neighboring ones. When they did demolish it, the people
who lived on those streets were not the same as those who
had lived there before the war. Africans, packed into
"foyers," and North Africans, especially men who hung
out in sinister cafés—gloomy pictures, gloomy music,
gloomy faces—had replaced the former population.
Those people had vanished, maybe into the smoke of the
gas chambers, or maybe into wealthier neighborhoods.
Also, some had been shot for being in the Resistance, the
Communist Resistance. Plaques affixed to the walls of
buildings recalled their names. When the buildings are
destroyed, the plaques will also disappear. So little would

remain of the names then—perhaps a few jottings in a book, or in a memoir—and soon they'd be rubbed out forever.

In those days you entered the café on rue Bisson. The tenants of the building thought of the owners as their friends. All the tenants were Jews, because the street was Jewish, as was the neighborhood, like in Warsaw. But the owners of the café were French, "real" French. During the war, as soon as the curfew was enforced, Jews in the building would gather in the café behind closed doors and play cards or dominoes. Like in Warsaw.

The Tenenbaums had lived in the building since arriving in France, their new homeland, from now on their only homeland, more home than Poland had ever been, for it had never really been home. Because the others wouldn't allow it, and because they themselves hadn't wanted it very much.

On July 16, 1942, at four in the morning, Rivka woke up her youngest daughter. The oldest, Esther, hadn't come home, hadn't slept at home that night. She would have been severely reprimanded by the father even though she was engaged, and to a very respectable young man, and even though she was an adult and over twenty-one. But the father. . . . What father?

Where was Uncle Avrum in those days? I don't know. He had joined the Polish army in France two years earlier, been taken prisoner by the Germans somewhere near the Somme, and had escaped. Do you know how? He pretended to have an attack of dysentery and asked to go to the latrines. A guard brought him over, and Uncle Avrum shoved him into the ditch. In the time it took for the guard to climb back out, Avrum was gone. Like a Chaplin movie, isn't it?

During the summer of 1942, Uncle Avrum is likely to

be at home, peacefully, in Belleville, like the others. Waiting to be picked up, to be told to pack his bags. To be told that he's lived long enough, that his time has come, this is the way it is, orders are orders. For him as for everyone else. Therefore, he's home, at his sewing machine, as always, as before, like the others.

Fanny listened to her mother without asking questions. You don't ask your mother questions. When her mother says something, she knows why she says it. She doesn't know everything, far from it, but what's good for Fanny, yes, *that* her mother knows. Fanny climbed up to the seventh floor, dressed as she was, in her underwear. And at the very moment that she was knocking, timidly, at the door of M. and Mme Dumur, she heard them knocking on doors on the floors below, and not so timidly. Rivka, Fanny's mother, didn't really think they would take women and children, what a crazy idea! But she thought that they had to be careful, take every precaution, you never know. Now, we know. Today, we know. We know, for example, that it wasn't manpower they were looking for. That they already had more than enough manpower. Consequently, what they *needed* were women and children. Because, according to plan, women and children were by no means destined for manpower. But you can never be too careful, thought Rivka, who didn't know everything, but who knew that you never know.

Rest assured, for why should you worry, that Fanny in her underwear had time to climb the four floors that separated the Tenenbaums from the Dumurs. Time. That's what mattered to Jews in those days—time. For other people, time, even in those days, was ordinary time. They had to wait it out, that's all. They had to wait for time to pass, to flow as usual, as time always passes when there's no hurry, when there's no fire, until the war was over. Wait for victory. For victory, for instance, why not victory? And whose victory, what victory? Take the prisoners of war; it was even forbidden to make them work, so they also waited. They didn't make love to their wives, they didn't see their children, but they could get news, yes, and packages. They were waiting. A little like being in prison, granted, but you could breathe and you had your pals. And if Uncle Avrum hadn't been such a big hero, he would have remained a prisoner of war, dysentery or no dysentery. Because at Auschwitz there were no debonair guards to accompany you to the latrines and exchange cigarettes, or small talk about children, or pass you crumpled sepia photos. He would have gone to Germany like the others, in torn clothes, moth-eaten cap, and shitkicker boots, and as Jewish as he was, the odds were that he'd return weighing more than a scarecrow. But no, he had to escape, had to shove his paterfamilias guard into the shithole, harmless shit though it was, while he, Avrum, sped head first toward this place he never heard of, that we could refer to politely as the *anus mundi*. Bad move. Stupid idiot.

And the mothers who had trouble feeding their children (what a terrible time), they had to wait. To wait for better days, for less dreary days: some waiting for the *Boches* to be kicked out of France—ah, De Gaulle—Joan of Arc—and others to be rid, once and for all, of the warmongering Jews, and other such cosmopolitan rabble. And couples who now were separated also had to wait. In ordinary time, even if that time was not ordinary. Yet even those days were not so extraordinary that time itself was topsy-turvy, or that day didn't follow night, or summer follow winter. Not so extraordinary. But for the Jews, those were extraordinary days. The Nazis had declared and enforced this decree: NO MATTER HOW the war would end, Europe would be cleansed of all the Jews, disinfected. So, for them, what did waiting mean?

As soon as the war ended, it was space that, for Jews, became different than for other people. At least, for those from the East. The village or the neighborhood where they had grown up was henceforth *judenrein*, "cleansed" of their presence. Often a survivor ended up alone in the world. While the others went home, could go home at last, the surviving Jews no longer had a home. Each parcel of earth where they were born was drenched in Jewish blood. They wouldn't think of treading on that soil again, the same earth that was once again flowering, being fertilized by the bones, the very ashes, of their relatives, their parents, their children. So he could choose to go to Western Europe, or to the United States, or "go up" to Palestine.

Do you remember Paris, on July 16, 1942, at four in the morning? It was already daylight. From the window of the Dumur apartment, Fanny looked out at rue Bisson and a bit of rue des Couronnes. She insists that she saw no Germans. She saw no buses. The French police at the crossroads were taking people away on foot.

I suppose that Uncle Avrum was sleeping that very morning, that very hour. He's not worried; his name isn't on the lists. Therefore he's asleep. So is Toba his wife. Despite the season, they're buried under the thick, white comforter. They're snoring, whistling like locomotives, happy, cradled, and they won't leave, not yet; only a dream carries them away, far away, perhaps to Poland where they come from, to Warsaw, to Panska Street. And from under the paunch of their comforter, they don't quite know what's afoot there, in Warsaw, in the Ghetto. What exactly is this ghetto they've laid out? What's really happening there at this very moment, mid-July in 1942? Worse than here? How could that be? The question, another question, really the question of questions, the one that subsumes all others. Mathieu has brought it up often with Simon P, his brother-in-law, since he started writing; and each time, as Charles would say, something gets stuck, gets blocked, and he no longer understands. So he forgets that he's already asked this question, that they've already talked about it. A question, in truth, so much debated since then, so often posed, scrutinized, argued, counter-argued, endless and monotonous as the obsessive sound of the sealed wagons on the tracks, and the same *oy* reflected on the concealed faces within, faces already broken, predicting what will happen to them in a few days, further East from here, in a place called *Pitchipoi* in the language of those faces— name of a place outside the law, a place expelled from the body of human law through the anus, where the law no longer applies, unheard-of excrement, nameless until then, group portrait in the cubist style, entanglement of corpses that the special prisoners, the *Sonderkommando* slaves, will untangle with the help of hooks, hoisting the bodies closer, to strip them further, to render them yet more naked, more like a mineral, because this was their job, to work the corpses. With the aid of hooks.

Simon P, whose parents had traveled that road, had walked the Street of Heaven—*Himmelstrasse*—belonged to an intermediary generation between Mathieu and his parents, and represented, he figured, the person most able to explain things: How could the Jews have let themselves be led away in this manner? Without flinching, without resisting? Let yourself be led away, for instance, by a French policeman, an officer not a bit Nazi, a good-natured policeman, easygoing as this simple *Wehrschutz* who accompanied Uncle Avrum to the latrines of his prison camp in the Somme, and who was so easily knocked down, thrown to the ground, even lower than the ground, into the latrines. And this policeman, the head of a family, nice, honest, moral—moral, yes, moral—not necessarily a fan of Wagner's music, but moral and honest. A policeman, a French officer, for instance, who through some goodness, charity, humanity, sometimes went so far as to warn his Jew that he would fetch him the next morning, asking him to get ready, to pack his suitcase, his bags, his traveling clothes, whatever. But who also let him understand that it was possible not to get ready, not to wait for him, the policeman, that it was up to him to disobey and clear out and escape to wherever he wanted, or could. But obedience, yes obedience, obey the law, most important of all, obey the law. What could possibly happen to you if you obeyed the law? What could they reproach you with? What sin, what infraction? But I obeyed the law, officer, look, I registered right away. Here's my identity card stamped with the word "Jew"! As for the officer, his job stopped there; he went to the house of his Jew, notified him that he's on the list, and was ready to take him away. And that's all. Now, if the person happened not to be home, it wouldn't be his responsibility. He had duly climbed the stairs, list in hand, knocked at the door announcing himself as specified in the police by-laws—the police prides itself on having and applying by-laws, the republican police force is proud of that—and inspected the apartment. His job was done. As for the rest, other functionaries would take it from there; he had done his part in the relay, passed on the baton, completed his mission dutifully, by the book, with honor and dignity—courtesy even—without shoving and pushing, in an orderly way. Order, *Ordnung*, the

144

others call it. *In Ordnung! Ordentlich!* But smoothly, correctly, without violence, what the hell, we are Frenchmen and not barbarians. Republican traditions oblige. So, what did Simon think? To let yourself be led away by such a French officer, to accept from the hands of a Pole, a Ukrainian, a Latvian, a Lithuanian, or even another Jew, a piece of soap, or perhaps a towel—I suppose it was a towel, and I can only suppose since I wasn't there—to take these as patent signs that you were indeed going to take a shower? What else could it have meant if not a shower, especially after those days and nights of traveling, traveling in urine, vomit, shit and sweat, above all sweat, *schwitz*, sweat, *schwitz*, emphasizing one of the two syllables of the unnameable toward which the trains were leading them.

Did Esther, like Mathieu, come to loathe traveling, and train stations?

And there, in Paris, in this July of 1942, the Jews were wondering: Why do the Germans want women and children? Of what use can women and children be to them? What useful work, war work, for instance, can women and children do? Yes, commented Simon, in those days logic wasn't the same for Jews as for other people. For the others, logic, even in those days, was ordinary logic. Not for the Jews. For the Jews, in those days, logic was new, unheard of, a logic people spent years, later, trying to understand. Yes, but a logic nevertheless. And even the *nec plus ultra* of logics. A logic that outclasses all other logics. A mechanical logic. See, in the ghettos, said Simon, the Jewish Council decided to turn over ten Jews out of a hundred to save ninety. Then, ten other Jews to spare the remaining eighty. What's more important, to sacrifice ten Jews or to save eighty? Then, as the German demands became even more pressing, the council delivered ten more Jews to the *Umschlagplatz* in order to save seventy. Logical. Then when only ten Jews were left, the Germans came and took them away. These last ten Jews were the members of the council. There weren't ten Jews left to take care of them, so the Germans themselves accomplished this little task. Further subtractions were performed. The Jews had been perfect accountants. Jews learned logic from the Greeks a long time ago. The Germans taught them order. Their aptitude for learning was nothing short of astounding!

But, for instance, asked Mathieu: How could a herd of four hundred Jews guarded by two SS, only two SS, allow themselves to be led toward what they knew was not a labor camp? Because, really, even without weapons, if they had suddenly scattered into the woods, even under the risky fire of the SS, of only two SS men, at least half of them would have escaped.

"You said it yourself," Simon proposes. "You weren't dealing with four hundred Jews but with a herd of four hundred Jews. At this point in the process, they were nothing more than a herd. And, besides, didn't you see how not only four hundred but two thousand Soviet soldiers led by the same two SS, these two lone SS, behaved in the same way, their shoulders hunched, passively entering the camp? Why would Jews have behaved differently, more admirably than these Soviet soldiers— soldiers with no illusions about the fate that awaited them?"

For Mathieu this was the real question, that of the victims' passivity, indeed their complicity with the torturers in their extermination. The true question was not the grandiose nonsense about the "silence of God." That particular silence did not constitute a question. Nor was it the silence of men. The question, the only one, was that

of the silence of the victims themselves. The silence of the
Jews facing the gas chamber. The silence of the Jews one
yard away from the gas chamber. The cry of the Jews
burst out only after the doors had been shut. But it was
a mute cry. The SS could *see* them cry out through the
peephole, but could not hear them. A mute cry. How can
a cry be mute? Three positions define us, a Hasidic rabbi
is rumored to have said when asked what constituted a
real Jew: to kneel standing up, to cry without voice, to
dance standing still . . .

"So, what's your conclusion?" asked Simon. "Do you
mean to say that it's in the gas chamber that Jews granted
this rabbi his wish?"

"No, I have no conclusion," said Mathieu. "It's only a
story . . ."

O

Simon told the following story: in a camp whose name
escapes me now, some Soviet soldiers were led to the barracks containing the showers. Now these happened to be
real showers. But since, for those prisoners, showers
meant gas, at a signal by one of them the entire group
ran and threw themselves on the electrified barbed wire.
They were all killed. As they died, they burst out screaming. As for the Jews, from them came a "cry without
voice."

Yet on this July 16, 1942, there were cries heard in
Paris, and they were heart-rending. When they grew
more sparse, Fanny sneaked out of the Dumur apartment
and ran down the stairs, bumping into her mother who
was coming up to meet her. She couldn't stay there. She
was to go hide in the shed of M. Dawidowicz, the butcher,
as planned.

Fanny crossed rue Bisson, and rushed through the main entrance of the building where the Dawidowiczes lived. But only their youngest daughter, Ginette, was at home. Together they ran to the butcher's shed and waited for a while, listening for noises. When everything was perfectly calm, they went out. From the street, Fanny called out to her mother, who threw her a jacket and a large bundle of clothes, and signaled for her to leave.

The girl tore off the yellow star from the jacket Rivka had thrown her, placing the strap of her pocketbook over the seam it had exposed. Then she walked toward the Couronnes station. Coming out of the metro on Boulevard Sebastopol, she went up to her friend Faigele Kurtz's apartment. She knocked. No one there. She went back down to ask the concierge, who whispered, the Kurtzes—which Kurtzes? Oh, yes, the Jews—they were on the seventh floor. There Fanny noticed Faigele the redhead among a dozen unfamiliar people. The place wasn't safe. The Kurtzes had friends in the suburbs. Fanny could come with them. No, they didn't mind, of course not, what was she saying?

The next morning Fanny telephoned her mother from the suburban town whose name escapes her now. Or rather telephoned the café at 27, rue des Couronnes.

That same morning, the morning of July 17, 1942, Rivka was waiting in the café at the corner of rue Bisson and rue des Couronnes, waiting for two phone calls— one from Fanny and one from Esther. Especially for the one from Esther. She had to avoid coming home like the plague. A police inspector had come the night before to warn the Tenenbaums that their two daughters had to be ready the next day with their personal belongings. On the morning of July 17, 1942, Fanny was the first one to call. The older daughter did not telephone. As Rivka had feared, she just showed up at home that morning, and had to leave with her mother and the police inspector who happened to be there. Good timing, in a way. Her name was on the list.

"Fanny? Here's your mother, I'll put her on."

Rivka took the receiver.

"Freydla," she said, "you must be brave. You are all alone now. You know that your father is sick. He left, he changed his address. As for me, I'm going away. I'm leaving with your sister. Take good care of yourself."

From that day on, Fanny had a suspicion that perhaps it had been her own name that had been on the list, and not that of her mother or her sister. In either case, either way, either her mother or her sister had been taken instead of her. With Fanny absent, the father absent, it was the extra woman, Rivka or Esther, who would have to do. Like in Warsaw. In Warsaw during the great *Aktion* of that same summer of 1942, the policemen needed a quota of heads. A certain number of heads, any heads at all, as long as they were Jewish heads. With this shade of difference, that in Warsaw the police hunting Jewish heads were themselves Jewish heads that other Jewish heads would hunt not long afterward. And, nuance within nuance, the prey of these head hunters who were deluded into thinking they were saving their own heads, was, sooner or later, their own families.

But we were in Paris, not in Warsaw. In the long run the result was the same, but not in the same manner. Right, not the manner. No question but that it was more neatly done in France.

"You see, she's a young woman," Rivka was able to tell the inspector, speaking of her oldest daughter Esther, or of Fanny. "I don't know what she's up to. She didn't sleep home last night. Perhaps she went dancing?"

Because, Fanny, like her sister, loved dancing. Passionately. It was at the dancehall in Lyon that some months later she really fell in love with Adek Litvak, I mean Charles, Charles who didn't come there to dance but to warn the Jewish youth not to hang out in this place because they could be picked up any time . . .

It just so happened that a cousin of Faigele Kurtz was a professional smuggler of people. The next morning, along with twenty other people, the Kurtzes and Fanny Tenenbaum crossed the Vichy line. The convoy stopped at Vierzon, right in front of the station, and immediately some men climbed the train at both ends and began asking people for their papers. Faigele Kurtz's cousin, the smuggler, kept his wits and ordered them all to remove their shoes and jump from the train down to the railroad bed. They were all to meet later in the café on the square of the village that could be seen not far away. Mme Kurtz then noticed that her husband had disappeared. She asked around about him. He had gone to the head of the train "to see what was happening." Mme Kurtz wanted to wait for him but her nephew, the smuggler, ordered her to jump. "I'll go find out," he said.

Fanny jumped from the train, lost her shoes, and, since she had to hurry, didn't look for them.

At last, the smuggler joined them at the café. Maurice had been arrested. He'd been asked for his papers. They hadn't been returned to him. "How stupid can you be," said the cousin-smuggler.

They waited for evening. Then hid on a truck under a tarpaulin, lying down flat, one against the other. The truck went through a thicket. A child cried. They drove two or three kilometers. Jumped. Fled across fields without stopping, without looking back, as the driver had instructed them. They heard gunshots in the distance, gunshots seemingly fired without conviction, haphazardly. They went up to peasants who let them stay in a stable, gave them something to drink. And didn't say, as in Poland, a thousand zlotys or else . . . and once having received the thousand zlotys, five thousand zlotys or else, et cetera . . . But it's a fact that French peasants, or the French in general, were not anti-Semites in the way that the Poles were; it's because the Germans, for reasons of their own, didn't need them to be: they hadn't deemed it opportune. They had plenty of time as far as the French Jews were concerned, all the time in the world; they were rather busy now with those from the East, the millions to "be taken care of" had top priority. It is not, it is especially not, as it has been said, because in France some Jews could hide, and be hidden, that such a great number of them were not exterminated. It's simply because the Germans had not yet decided.

Fanny arrived in Lyon with the Kurtzes. In her socks. Strange, says Mathieu, this business of lost shoes. When Avrum, his mother's uncle, came back from Auschwitz via Odessa, his feet were covered with newspapers. So what? asked Simon P. So nothing, said Mathieu, it's strange, that's all.

In Lyon, the Kurtzes found rooms in an old hotel filled with Jews. The heat was unbearable. For Fanny, the first night spent in this filthy place was hell. She shared Faigele's room and bed. She woke her up in the middle of the night.

"I don't know what's the matter with me," she told her, "I'm covered with blood. I'm covered with blood from head to toe. My hands are full of blood; I have blood on my hands."

Faigele turned on the light: Fanny was covered with bedbugs.

"I can't sleep here. I'm going out in the street."

"I have a good friend," said Faigele. "His room is on the third floor. He's very sweet. He'll put you up for tonight. But you'll have to share a bed."

They went down the rickety hotel stairs in the dark, and Faigele Kurtz explained the situation to her friend who wanted, above all, to go back to sleep. But he didn't fall back asleep. Not right away: dragged from his sleep, when he made out the young girl's features he woke up completely.

His name was Adek. Adek Litvak. That is, his name was Charles. She should call him Charles. Charles was actually his name. He had been living in the Free Zone for more than a year. Because he was a boy his aunt, Shoshe, after the first roundups of Jews in Paris in 1941, had been afraid for him. Otherwise, he was from Warsaw. His parents, meaning his mother, his sister Guta, his brother Bolek, were in Warsaw. Perhaps still in Warsaw. Perhaps still alive. He wasn't sure. His oldest brother Nathan, the sculptor, was able to flee to Russia, to Moscow. His father, Yankel, had died a few years before the war. Since he didn't want to continue with school, they had sent him to Paris, to his aunt and uncle in Belleville. And his Aunt Shoshe had had the instinct to send him to a peasant, in Haute-Savoie, you never know.

You never know. There were camps in France in those days. Not death camps. But camps. At that time, no one heard of death camps. The word itself did not exist. Because the thing had never existed. At no time in history, at any latitude. The Germans invented the word and the thing. It was surprising. Didn't Simon think it surprising that it had never existed before? Such a simple thing. Yes, but that's precisely what genius does, it invents things that are very simple. And around 1942, that's what

the Germans were, geniuses! There had been camps before, granted, granted. And slaughters, of course, of
course. But slaughters in camps? Slaughters in a confined
place, conceived solely for that purpose, organized, ra-
tional? That did not exist before. This notion of "death
camp" had not existed. No one had yet invented it. The
Germans, let's give them credit, are the ones who had
the genius to do it. Already they had shown a genius for
music and for philosophy. They had the added genius to
invent the "death camp." Concerns about the gas and
ovens, and what Zyklon B was made of, and the complicated plumbing, or whether the tiles really made it look
like a shower, these don't really matter. What matters
is the principle: the industrialization of death. Such a
principle would have been inconceivable to barbarians,
to the most barbarous of barbarians. The pale-faces
couldn't have thought of it for the redskins, or the con-
quistadors for the Indians, or the Turks for the Armeni-
ans: no conqueror could have conceived of it for any
conquered people. Because in order to invent a "death
camp," one had precisely *not* to be a barbarian. One had
to know philosophy and music. One had to be German.
I see no other way. Does Simon see another way? No,
Simon sees no other way, either. Just as the Jews invented
God, the Germans invented the death camp. They invented the death camp deliberately to exterminate the
Jews who invented God. What exactly did they want to
exterminate—God, or the people who invented Him? It
leads you to believe that the Germans, who had a genius
for music and philosophy, had on top of that a genius
for theology, and that the "death camp" in principle is
perhaps nothing more than a discourse on God, and the
most radical one there is.

○

Charles was fully awake now. He liked this girl. She, for her part, didn't seem to dislike him. She listened to him carefully, wanted him to speak of Warsaw, of his childhood, of his family. Which he did, hesitating at first, but then opening up, as if unburdening himself to an old friend, almost an alter ego.

○

Our street, said Charles, the one where I was born, was a tiny little street, more like a narrow alley that opened onto a large square crowded with Jews. All the buildings looked like this hotel, just as rundown and as crammed with Jews. The street was called Mylna, a deceptive street. My real first name isn't Charles, but Adek. It really isn't Adek either, but Abraham. The name on my birth certificate is Abraham Litvak. They changed Abraham to Adek to simplify things. And not to make it sound more Polish? asked Fanny. Yes, you're right, to make it sound more Polish. Not so much to simplify things. But still, in a way, to simplify things. For the same reasons that my name is now Charles. You're going to ask: Why Charles? Why not Charles?

I was told that when I was born the house was full of flowers. It seems that they threw a party for my circumcision that lasted three days and three nights. Maybe it's true. There were lots of people, there was dancing.

Until I left at fourteen for my Aunt Shoshe's, we had moved five or six times. I'll tell you about those changes of address so that you'll know Warsaw, at least that part of Warsaw. We never moved very far . . .

My parents were manufacturers of ladies' hats. One

day, I don't know why, they lost their business; they went bankrupt. Then we became poor. My father, Yankel, gave up all responsibility, so my mother, Raisl, ran the house. Then Yankel fell ill. He never got over it. That's called a nervous breakdown.

They turned me over to Mme Goldberg, a friend of Guta, my oldest sister. I spent two years with the Goldbergs. Two wonderful years, the best part of my childhood in Warsaw, perhaps of my life. The Goldberg house was orderly; they led a normal life. I went to *heder*, you know, the Jewish elementary school. I received presents for my birthday. I was so happy that I used to sing as I ate. I used to sing while eating.

"You must not sing while eating," M. Goldberg said.

"And why not?" I asked.

"Because later, you risk having a mute wife . . ."

Frightened, I stopped singing.

The Goldbergs honored traditions and the Torah. Passover was the most beautiful of all Jewish holidays. Even today, twenty-two years old, when I have trouble, I still think of the Goldbergs, of their house on Nowolipki Street. When I was depressed at my aunt's house in Belleville, it wasn't so much my family that I thought of but the Goldbergs. I would lie down on the couch and tell myself: now I am at the Goldbergs', as before, as before. You see, it made me feel better.

Mathieu stopped on the words "as before." "Before," he thought, was for Charles, his father, even in those days, when neither Esther or Mathieu were born yet, when little or nothing was known about what would be learned afterward, "before" was still an ordinary word, as "before" was for you, or me. A moment, a privileged, slightly mythical time, no doubt, in our childhood. Before, in other words. But later, after we learned, *before* meant what preceded the Catastrophe, the *Shoah*. The absolute before. Followed by an absolute afterward. This interval—a second, a point, an instant in time—exists only because we know that it was preceded by a before and was followed by an afterward (every day, people die who knew that there was a before; every day since then, children are born who learn through books and movies that there was a before). This instant in time, this nothingness, is called Auschwitz. Auschwitz is the name of this nothingness. This "nothingness" is very much like God. Perhaps it is his ultimate name. Like him it is useless. Like him it is unimaginable and transcends us. Like him, it cannot be proved: some people doubt the existence of Auschwitz, or, on the contrary, attempt to prove its existence just as foolishly as others try to prove God exists. Like God, Auschwitz is not deniable; it's just as foolish to prove the nonexistence of God as it is that of gas chambers. In the divine plan, the Jews, apex of humanity, received God. According to the human project, Auschwitz, apex of humanity, received the Jews.

"So what's your conclusion?" asked Simon.

"Nothing, I have no conclusion," repeated Mathieu. "It doesn't matter . . ."

O

Charles continues:

The Goldbergs owned a curious radio receiver. You could only hear it through earphones. We each had our own, glued to our ears. At night we would listen to classical music, piano music, Chopin, interpretations of Paderewski, the virtuoso, the dandy. The only presents I got as a child, at least the only ones I can remember, came from the Goldbergs. The first present was a pair of ice skates, from Sweden. The Goldbergs were rich. Do you know what Goldberg means? Mountain of gold. They were rich. They lived on Nowolipki. Careful, not Nowolipie—Nowolipki. Nowolipki Street was very different from Mylna Street, much nicer, broader. Almost all the Jews there spoke Polish. You could breathe there; it didn't smell as bad.

I hated the *heder*. When I made a mistake, the rabbi wouldn't hesitate to hit me across the fingers with a big ruler. I hated it. Me, little Adek who spoke Polish, spoiled by the Goldbergs, mountain of gold, comforter, classical music, ice skates from Sweden if you please, Passover feast, what was I doing with this slightly dirty rabbi who smelled of onions and hit me on the fingers with his ruler, as if I were a penniless child whose parents couldn't say a thing?

O

Jews fought in all the armies that were fighting the Nazis, and bravely, Mathieu thought to himself. But the most important fight, the most useful, was the fight of Jews to save the children, the greatest number of children possible. These struggles didn't take place within the same dimensions of time. The first transpired in ordinary time, ordinary logic. The other pertained to a time of urgency, to the logic of catastrophe. Soon no one would be left who had been alive during the catastrophe. Not a single Jew left.

Simon P's story:

In what book was it? One day, quite a while after the war, a Jew goes back, as a tourist, to visit the camp to which he had been deported. Each day, some years before, the *Häftlinge* were gathered in groups of five and led to a certain place to do grueling work for twelve hours. On their way, they would walk by a farm at the edge of a small market town. And the peasants and their blond children, perhaps *Volksdeutsche*, would watch the column of ghosts walk by. So, this Jew took the same path on foot again, walked by the same small town, stopped in front of the farm and asked the farmers if they had been there during the war. Yes, they had never left the place. Did they remember these hundreds of shaved skulls, striped pajamas, wooden clogs walking by, twice a day, back and forth, singing a Polish marching tune? No, they absolutely had no memory of that. They had never seen groups of striped pajamas. Except once, on television. He must be mistaken.

There you have it, said Mathieu. Between this Jewish "tourist," this strange "tourist" asking strange questions, and this Polish peasant whose good faith I would not doubt, there is a gap. What kind of a gap? A lapse of memory? A million books telling the story of that camp would not be enough to fill the gap, to make that Pole find his memory again.

○

Mylna, Nowolipki. Then it was Bonifraterska Street, Charles continued. M. Goldberg used to take me around Warsaw on Sundays, on the Z streetcar, the one that zigzagged like a Z through Warsaw. On the streetcars Poles would look at the Jews, stare at their profiles to see if they were Jewish. When they recognized a Jew they would yell, "it smells of onions here!" They called us "cats" or "Bedouins."

Mme Goldberg, I just remembered, was born Zlotagora, imagine that. In Polish that means mountain of gold. So, she had the same name as her husband, Goldberg. Besides, they were both rich, as if by design.

Across from us, on Bonifraterska Street, was a school, a wooden building. And then a large square where boys played soccer before and after classes.

After Bonifraterska, there was Nalewki. A main street crowded with Jews. I saw very little of my brother Bolek; he was ten years older than me. But the oldest was Nathan. My sister Guta, the oldest, was studying medicine at the University of Warsaw. Me, I was the *muzhinkl*, the baby of the family.

Bolek had found work in the Zionist office. But he was a Communist. Nathan, who was connected with *Hashomer Hatzair*, the left-wing Zionists, had gotten him this job. But Bolek wasn't comfortable there. He didn't care for Zionists, be they left, right, or centrist. Since he didn't hide his internationalist convictions, it stirred up conflicts. Nathan suggested he hold his tongue: *Shhhh!*

At home on Nalewki Street, no money. How would they manage for *Shabbes* without money? The question came up every Thursday, every week . . .

And then Pawia Street. Our windows opened on the Pawiak prison. Since we lived high up, we could see the prisoners line up every morning at dawn. They used to sing. The song of the Pawiak prisoners woke us up every morning. They always sang the same refrain, I forgot which one.

I changed schools, left the one on Bonifraterska Street, next to the soccer field, for one on Ptachia Street, the street of birds. They spoke Polish at that school but the students and teachers were all Jewish. The very dirty courtyard, which also served as a marketplace, held barrels of herring. When I used to come home, Raisl would comment on the smell. But it wasn't my fault, I used to protest, it was the herring of Ptachia Street! I didn't like school, neither that one nor another. I never had all my books: my parents couldn't afford to buy them all for me. I had only one pair of shoes. When they had worn out, Raisl would write me a note, saying that I was sick, and I would spend the morning at the shoemaker's, which wasn't any worse than school.

O

Fanny Tenenbaum's eyes blinked, and she turned her face toward the window. It was the depth of night. What would tomorrow bring?

O

When Yankel, my father, lost his hat business, he never got over it. He was *kaput*. He didn't leave his bed, only to lie down on the couch. Did he read? Did he daydream? Like a deranged and harmless golem he gave orders that nobody paid any attention to. Was he grumbling because no one respected him? Or, resigned, did he simply accept his fate?

O

(Yankel, the hatmaker, Charles's father, in Mathieu's "novel," his "novel" about the ghetto, will see his fate transferred to the character of Charles himself. His store in the Aryan Zone will be confiscated, and from then on he'll remain prostrate on the bed or couch, giving up the fight, even the desire to live. But perhaps he'll bounce back, want to "save his skin," and, in ultimate cowardice, abandon his family to hide in the Polish Zone. As for Raisl, she'll be Fanny; she'll die of exertion, or of sickness, or will be deported during the great *Aktion* in the summer of 1942, this very summer, almost the same day that Fanny and Charles actually met.)

O

Charles went on: my mother's maiden name was Kapelowicz. You couldn't find a better name for someone who sold hats. When Yankel fell "ill," Raisl contacted his former clients and sold them merchandise she bought from the manufacturers. All week long, she traveled back and forth from Warsaw. On the eve of *Shabbes*, she always managed to bring back food—sausage, eggs, cheese.

And this was on Nowolipie Street. Not Nowolipki, careful: Nowolipie. I must have been around ten. Once again, only Jews lived in our building. Our room was huge; we even thought of fixing up a corner to sublet, although we ourselves were subletting from a tenant. We put a sign up at the door: "Room for rent for an intelligent student."

Charles laughed.

We were poor, we had nothing, we lacked everything, but we wanted the student to be intelligent!

On the eve of *Shabbes*, Raisl would empty her purse on the table. And all of us would count the money, piling up coins in big stacks, in little stacks, carefully, quietly, sorting bills in wads of ten, which we would secure with a straight pin. It's my mother who taught me how to wet my thumb to count bills while holding them folded a certain way in my hand.

(Much later, in the storage room in back of his father's shop, Mathieu would be fascinated by his father's confident, "professional" gestures. You sure have a lot of money, he would tell him. And Charles would answer: you know, in business, the money you count isn't necessarily your own. Sometimes it's the money you owe . . .)

The money we used to count before *Shabbes*, Charles went on, at home in Warsaw, at 42 Nowolipie Street, wasn't our own money, don't worry, it was the money we owed, the money that my mother owed her suppliers. They would come for it a few days later. And when they came, we were always a little short. In spite of all of Raisl's efforts, there was never quite enough to pay the debts. Sometimes my mother cried. Always so that Yankel wouldn't see. Nathan, my older brother, had to provide for our needs—which bothered him; he would complain. He didn't live with us, but in student housing, in Praga. He studied at the Beaux-Arts.

We had no electricity at home. We used gas for light . . . small bulbs so fragile they would explode if you so much as touched them. When the lights dimmed, you had to put another coin in a meter on the landing. We didn't always have the fifty groszy. But Raisl proved very resourceful. Every month, or every other month, when the man from Poland Gas would come, he'd open the box on the landing to collect the coins.

"See here, Madame Litvak," he would say, pushing his cap back on his head, "what's happening here? I have coins from all over the world, all sorts of coins, all sorts except the right kind, the fifty groszy! What are you doing? And what am I going to do, what can I do with that now? Coins from all over the world, all over. But not the fifty groszy."

Charles laughed.

Fanny Tenenbaum laughed.

He's not boring her with all these stories? Did she want to go to sleep?

But Fanny was already asleep, she fell asleep all of a sudden, like a child.

○

Toward the end of 1941, at the time of the first round-ups of Jews, Charles's aunt, Shoshe, borrowed five thousand francs, found a smuggler, and sent her nephew to the Haute-Savoie. Before going to the peasant who had agreed to take him in (and to employ him), Charles stopped for a while at Lyon, to visit distant relatives on his mother's side. They were people who had emigrated from Warsaw a few years earlier. They were Hasidim, pious Jews, with beards. Their apartment in Lyon didn't have heat but at least they had thick Polish-style comforters. Their place, Charles remembers, was very dirty. And especially dangerous: these long, white beards weren't exactly invisible.

○

Simon P's story:
In the Warsaw Ghetto the Hasidim hardly ever left their rooms, so as to remain pious, to keep their beards and earlocks. They said it was their way of resisting. Yet others, less intransigent, or having different views about how to safeguard their Jewishness, hid their features and tried to get over to the Aryan side. There they simply had to avoid unpleasant encounters with Poles who could denounce or blackmail them. In those days, the Poles had invented a new profession: blackmailing Jews . . .

○

Sporting Esther's oversized cap, Mathieu, who was growing a beard, went out into the streets with trepidation. Would somebody knock his hat off into the mud and force him to get off the sidewalk to pick it up, as had happened to Freud's father? No, nobody noticed him.

Unlike the Warsaw Jews who would have given a lot of money to cross over to the Aryan side, and who indeed gave a lot, Mathieu followed the path in the other direction, went from the Aryan side toward the ghetto. But how could he fail to notice that Paris had neither an Aryan side nor a ghetto? There's no war yet, he told himself. And he was reassured and disappointed. He had frightened himself for nothing. He was playing at frightening himself. When war breaks out again, he told himself, I'll go immediately to the United States.

The summer before her suicide, Esther went to New York. From what was she escaping? Wasn't going to New York that summer for her a circuitous way of getting to Poland without going there? In truth, wasn't it Poland that was calling her like a black spell? Perhaps by flying to New York, the biggest Jewish city in the world, she hoped to find signs of a vanished world that was still alive, a preserved world where Jews lived in ordinary time, spared, becoming what they had to become, what only time could make them become. Granted, they spoke less and less Yiddish, forgot little by little the life of their ancestors in Eastern Europe; but this distance, this separation, had not been forced on them, wasn't the result of war. Perhaps Esther told herself that the best way to hang on to these scraps of a bygone Jewish life was to cross the Atlantic and turn her back on Poland—where state museums could show her only pieces of flint, fossils, potsherds, and other bone fragments that once belonged to these strange, extinct animals, the Jews, who were said to have existed before the war. What a strange paradox, thought Mathieu, to seek the world of the past in the very city that augurs the world of tomorrow! Was Esther's trip fruitful? Several months later, they buried her. It's true that, in the meantime, Simon P had found another woman.

O

Charles remembers:
At home on Nowolipie Street, Charles said, our rent went up to seventy-five zlotys. The landlord, a Jew like us, lived in the same courtyard. Looking embarrassed and stroking his long salt-and-pepper beard, he came to collect his rent every month. Raisl always told him to come back next month.

At my Aunt Shoshe's house, whenever I had trouble, big trouble, I thought of the Goldbergs, of their house on Nowolipki Street. And my troubles would go away; I would be happy again. When some little thing bothered me, some trivia, I'd think about our own apartment on Nowolipie Street. It would hit me clear as day: What did I have to complain about?

You see, he said to Mathieu who was asking him questions, two houses away, on Nowolipie, there was a grocer.

"Adek," Raisl would order, "go do the shopping."

She would hand me a scribbled list. But no money.

When the grocer saw me, he'd take out his pencil and write everything down in a fat book: a hundred grams of butter, two hundred grams of sugar, *monczka*, flour . . . . And as the list was growing out of proportion, he'd say:

"You'll notify your mother that you've already got many pages in my book!"

What we owed left and right we no longer counted in zlotys, but in pages!

Charles is silent.

There was no hot water in the kitchen, he went on.

Silence once more. Has it to do with his talking? Has it to do with remembering?

Raisl was a very cheerful person. Always a funny story to tell. It will all work out, she would say. Or else, we'll manage, don't worry. . . .

But it didn't work out. She wound up without even a grave.

Her name was Raisl Kapelowicz. She sold hats in and around Warsaw. Always on the run, doing rounds, and her husband in bed, and no money, and the "pages" piling up.

And Mathieu's pages. Pages of debt, for him also. Irretrievable.

Kapelusz, in Polish, is a hat. Exactly. In those days we were all mad hatters. We were afraid of going mad. So we left.

O

One evening in the fall of 1942, in Lyon, in their common bed, Charles told Fanny that he would not go back to the peasants. He would stay with her. But Lyon was becoming too dangerous. They went to Grenoble. There, Charles ran into a Parisian acquaintance, a young man from Belleville. He belonged to the *Franc-Tireurs*, a partisan resistance movement, and he easily convinced Charles to join. So Charles disappeared. He saw Fanny only now and then. When Fanny realized that she was pregnant, she discussed it with Charles. They decided not to resort to abortion.

O

Uncle Avrum is going through his papers piled up on the dining-room table. He's taken everything out of the drawers. For me. Toba, his wife, sits facing me. She'll be present at the interview. Which bothers me slightly. It seems to me that I would have been more comfortable with Uncle Avrum only. Toba likes to talk a lot. She'll interrupt too often, sidetrack Avrum from his train of thought, speak in his stead.

He's searching feverishly through his papers, for what I don't know. Does he know himself? A date perhaps? I came to listen, simply to listen to him, once he had agreed. How do I dare ask a question? Coming was like diving into water. I'm not prepared. It's all too much.

He found it. Here it is. I was arrested November 19, 1942. Led to La Santé prison. I had broken the law.

Then, an endless silence.

Wait. He's looking through his papers. Shouldn't I have brought two recording tapes instead of one?

Toba breaks the silence. We hadn't declared ourselves as Jews. Avrum mimics anger. If you talk, then I can't talk. This little scene diffuses some of the tension. My tension, but not only mine.

I was charged with being an escaped prisoner, and when I was acquitted of that infraction, I was charged, once more, for not having registered as a Jew.

Silence.

Then, I was deported. I was deported . . .

Silence. It's not going well.

(Later Mathieu tells Simon P: So, you register as a Jew and you wind up on the list to be deported. You don't register, and you risk being arrested and deported for that very reason. But what can Mathieu pretend to teach

Simon, Simon whose parents had not come back? That's what it was about him that had seduced Esther, because, according to Mathieu, Simon P is a being lacking in charm.)

O

Esther was born on August 2, 1943. Charles went to City Hall to register the child. They had agreed to call her Rose, after Raisl, Charles's mother. When Charles returned, Rose's name was Esther. He couldn't very well call her Rebecca!

On my way over there, he later told Mathieu, something bothered me about giving my daughter my mother's name. For me, it would have been as though my mother were already dead, and, who knows, maybe she wasn't. Maybe a miracle had occurred. At that time I didn't know that Fanny's sister was named Esther. But I'm not absolutely sure. Maybe she had told me? I don't remember.

Mathieu assumes that he knew it, that Fanny had told him, and that in naming his daughter Esther, and not Rose, he was stacking the deck, a little magically perhaps, for his mother to have survived the war, and not to have been swallowed up in the ghetto. She might have been able to hide in some bunker, or in an attic, get out of the ghetto through a sewer, or reach the Aryan side, leave Warsaw and find refuge in the forest: anything was possible. And in sparing his mother's name, he had some small say in sparing her herself. In any case, he avoided doing anything to shorten her life, avoided making himself accomplice, yes, almost an accomplice to her death. And as for Fanny's sister, Esther, deported a year earlier from Drancy, may her soul rest in peace . . .

O

The day that Charles went to declare his daughter in City Hall, Uncle Avrum was at Birkenau, *Häftling*. About Birkenau, Avrum will tell Mathieu nothing. Or very little, just snatches, his speech becoming disjointed, and Mathieu too terrorized to interrupt, to ask.

At Birkenau, Avrum says, he met an acquaintance, a *landsman*, a fellow countryman. This man had people call him Moishe-Leyb Nietka, but his real name was Yankelewicz. Why this double identity? A mystery. Avrum was assigned to Block 19, which was run by an "anti-Semite, a Polack, a murderer." Yankelewicz came to see Avrum: "Here, you see," he told him, "there are four chimneys, one, two, three, four. If you stay longer at Birkenau, you'll be burned in one of those four chimneys. You'll be ashes in one of those four chimneys. A transport is leaving for a coal mine in Jaworzno. You'll go with it. As long as you are alive, you're alive."

This Yankelewicz had been in Birkenau for a long time. Here, Avrum said, his lot was more enviable than it had been in "civilian" life. Since he'd been able to resist all this time, the SS respected him. He was dressed like a prince. He belonged to the *Sonderkommando*. He collected the clothes. He had a harmonica, a tiny harmonica that he'd been able to hide. And he played it, Toba said as if she herself had seen and heard him, like a virtuoso. He played it for the Germans. German marches, Avrum explained. And because he had survived, and because he played the harmonica so well, the SS let him stay alive and gave him a task to perform. And there, if you had a duty to perform, you didn't lack for a bowl of soup. Me, I did without, but not others. Whoever could take a stick in his hand and right away start beating someone, that one had a chance to survive . . .

This isn't Mathieu talking. Especially not him. It's Uncle Avrum. Mathieu isn't talking. He's listening. He doesn't have the right to talk. Nor to have an opinion, put forward a hypothesis or a doubt, add something, or contradict or explain or say that he knows this or that, that he heard someone say, that he read. Even if you'd read *everything*, you'd still know *nothing*. He has the right to be quiet, to keep quiet. No opinion on "that." Especially no opinion. Nothing to say. The right to say nothing. There's nothing to think about. Nothing to see. Keep moving.

○

Charles's story:

My sister Guta was considered the most intelligent one in the family. That's what they said. Nathan paid for her studies at the university. He did this gladly, intending for her to become a *mensch*. But she disappointed him, and he didn't forgive her. As soon as she entered the university, she fell for a boy, Misha Peltzman, a handsome boy. They were married, she became pregnant right away, and had to give up her studies.

Each year, a few days before the first of May, the police would come to nab Bolek. They would release him soon afterward and he'd return with a beard. He was marked a Communist in their files. At home, we had clandestine meetings. We weren't very kosher. At night my mother would run off fliers on an old machine, as in books by Gorky.

I also dreamed of another world. When I was depressed, I'd go to the movies to see Errol Flynn or Johnny

Weissmuller. Sometimes I'd stay through two showings, four hours at a stretch. Perhaps, I told myself, some day I'd live a different life.

My grandfather was a great Talmudist. Isn't that what all Jews say? But it's true, he was, Charles insisted. He knew the Talmud like the back of his hand. So much so that the rabbis themselves came to consult Shmulik Litvak. On our street, on Nowolipie, I was known as the grandson of the *shoykhet*, the ritual slaughterer. He lived across the street from us. They said that he still made love to my grandmother, even though he was over eighty years old. Sometimes, before the Sabbath, my mother would give me a chicken for my grandfather to slaughter according to the ritual. For me, he would do it for nothing, of course.

The biggest thing he would reproach me for was not speaking Yiddish. Everyone spoke Yiddish at home, and I understood it. But I spoke Polish. When he wanted to make fun of me, or shame me, my grandfather would say: "So, say something in Yiddish . . ."

And I would get mixed up, and I couldn't. I spoke only Polish. Even here, in Paris, when I speak with Poles, they're very surprised:

"It's strange," they tell me, "you speak Polish like us, without an accent."

Even Yankel, my father, never learned to speak Polish. Never. When I arrived in France, what struck me was that for the most part, the French Jews spoke French correctly, like Frenchmen. In Poland, the Jews would butcher the language, which made the Poles very angry. The Jews lived only among themselves, spoke only Yiddish. Me, I was rather the exception. It's here in France that I actually learned Yiddish, in Belleville, at my Aunt Shoshe's. Because I didn't know French and they spoke

Polish too poorly. At first, they would make fun of me, asking me if I hadn't become a Catholic?

○

When Esther was born, Fanny moved to Domène, a few kilometers from Grenoble. She lived there under some sort of curfew, with an Italian landlady who didn't ask for much rent. After a while, Fanny called herself Simone Poulat. She even succeeded in misleading the Municipal Civil Service into giving her a fake identity card. That is, a *real* fake one. All things considered, Simone Poulat was better than Freydla Tenenbaum. The problem was that Fanny would stroll about with both of them, the real card that placed her in mortal danger and the fake one that vouched for her "frenchness." Had she been stopped and searched, she would have been arrested. Which is what almost happened to her one January day in 1944 while she was strolling with Esther in her baby carriage. Two men in civilian clothes accosted her, and asked if she knew someone by the name of Freydla Tenenbaum. No, she had never heard that name.

"We'll go see at City Hall," said one of the two policemen.

Fanny went back to the Italian landlady, bundled up Esther, and took the first bus to Sassenage where Mme Kurtz lived.

○

Uncle Avrum arrived at the Birkenau camp with a pharmacist from Nancy. The latter quickly understood the situation. His first gesture was to grab a stick and hit someone. Jews! Brothers! Toba screamed, animals, that's what they became there!

172

The privileged ones, Avrum went on, worked with the *Sonderkommando*, or in "Canada," the place where they sorted the possessions of the Jews. Like my Yankelewicz. He could wheel and deal. If he wanted a roasted chicken he could get it easily, and the same for alcohol. He could go from one camp to the other. He worked at sorting the clothes of Jews on their way to be gassed as soon as they stepped off the train. And every piece of clothing held a precious object, usually a diamond. Whether the convoy came from France, from Holland, from Hungary, from Czechoslovakia, or Greece, the Jews had had the same impulse to arm themselves with a precious stone.

He helped me, this Yankelewicz. Sometimes he would bring me a bowl of soup; he could move about. One day I went myself to get this bowl of soup, went to his block. Which cost me three teeth. His *Blockälteste*—that's what they called the block supervisors—a Polack, caught me and punched me in the jaw.

Yankelewicz, said Toba, died not long ago at Néris-les-Bains, where he was taking the waters.

He's the one, Avrum went on, who wanted me to go to the Jaworzno mines so that I wouldn't burn in one of the four ovens. Why? Because he was a *landsman*. His grandfather, his brother, all the Yankelewiczes, had worked for my grandfather.

One time, said Toba, your uncle is walking down Avenue Sécrétan. It was right after the war. And whom does he see? A former *Blockälteste*, but not from his block. This man was a murderer, says Avrum, one of the murderers of Birkenau, Block 5. M. Schafman he called himself. I didn't know that creature, adds Toba. Your uncle sees him and says to him: Where are you off to? He wanted to show him that he recognized him. And Mathieu asks, What was he, a German, a Pole? And Toba and Avrum, together: A YID! A YID!

In our mine at Jaworzno, our *Blockälteste* were, at first, German common criminals, green triangles. Then they were sent to the Russian front. So, to replace them they took a few *Blockälteste* from everywhere, from Birkenau, from Auschwitz. That's how Schafman became *Blockälteste* at Jaworzno. He lived on rue Saint-Antoine, said Toba. At one time it was forbidden to beat a *Häftling* at Jaworzno. They needed more coal. Every two weeks there was a selection. Those deportees who were too exhausted were gassed at Birkenau. In the mines there were some Ukrainians, some Poles. They had the right to receive packages. Not the Jews. Us, we had no right to anything.

This M. Schafman saved my life. Here's how. They used to hang people who sold their shirts. The kapos would inspect the blocks; the *Hemdlose*, those caught without their shirt, were hanged the next day. Me, I had sold my shirt for a piece of bread, down in the mine. And this M. Schafman got me a shirt, saving my life. Why, above all, did you need a shirt? To resist the bad weather. And the Germans had no more shirts to distribute. You had to hold out to produce for them. It was already the end. The end for them, but the end also for us. We knew that they'd kill us all, sooner or later, right before the end.

O

At the start of 1944 Fanny and Esther are in Sassenage, Charles is in Grenoble with the *Franc-Tireur* partisans. As for Uncle Avrum, he was sent to Warsaw to clean out the ghetto. Clear out the place. The ghetto has been liquidated for several months now. The Germans have fantastic plans for urban renewal. But first, everything must be razed. Jews from Auschwitz will do the job.

O

In Sassenage, Fanny catches up with her friend Faigele at Mme Kurtz's. Faigele was pregnant. Her "fiancé" and his mother were also there. Fanny had no money and no place to go. They were looking for her. Mme Kurtz had put her up as best she could. But it became clear that this little world simply couldn't get along, neither the "mothers-in-law" nor the fiancé and his mother. Neither Faigele and her future mother-in-law, nor Mme Kurtz and her future son-in-law, nor even Faigele and her fiancé. There was constant yelling. Esther's own contribution was the last straw.

Faigele decided Fanny couldn't stay. Her mother gave her a little money, enough to rent a hotel room. Once more, Fanny muffled up the baby and went out into the night, the cold and the snow.

In the streets she suddenly felt desperate. Rivka and Esther had been deported. Charles was God knows where. She gave up looking for a hotel. She huddled in the doorway of a house, slid to the ground, and, squeezing Esther against her, watched the snow fall. She thought of her father, Szymon, her only anchor. They wrote to each other regularly. When Fanny knew that she was pregnant and that she would keep the baby, she informed him at once. He took it well. It wasn't the end of the world. She was his daughter and would always remain his daughter, no matter what. He sent her a package of baby clothes, things knitted by hand, jumpers, an enormous box shipped by train. During that period, trains weren't used only to deport Jews. By the way, Szymon wrote, they had "taken" his brother Avrum, who had sent him word from Drancy. He was doing okay, he said, but had no news of Rivka and Esther. Szymon had warned him: You had to register. You had to obey the law. As long as Jews obeyed the law, no harm would come to them. . . . These remarks infuriated Fanny. And her mother and sister, hadn't they obeyed the law?

Even though I'd been afraid to question Uncle Avrum, and never would have thought of getting more from him, and the idea never entered my head to drag up *everything* that he knew, it nevertheless is true that, going home that night, I accused myself of being unprepared, of having been too cowardly; I was angry at myself for not having been up to it all, for having spoiled the interview. Then, later on, I told myself that I'd done right by my uncle, even if it had been unintentional, by not acting like a journalist trying to drain his witness to the very marrow. What he told me about Birkenau doesn't give me more than a general idea of the place. In his story I don't see him—Avrum—in Birkenau. Nor in the coal mine at Jaworzno. I don't see him prey to hunger, to beatings, to torture, to cold, to sickness. I don't see him in Warsaw either. I don't see anything. I cannot see anything. I don't want to see anything. I must not see anything. Wanting to see would place me alongside that SS man assigned to look through the peephole of the gas chambers at those being gassed.

O

It was because he still had some strength left that he, Avrum Tenenbaum, was chosen to go to the ghetto, after the Jews of the ghetto had been either deported or shot on the spot.

Avrum's story:

We left for Warsaw in the beginning of 1944. Our task was to blow up the houses. When there were no blocks to shelter us, we slept in the houses still standing. The Germans guarded us, taking roll in the morning and at night, like in the camp. To blow up the houses, we dug a hole in the basement and in the ceiling. Then, the *Meister*, a Polack, came and placed the explosives. We would leave the building and he'd blow it up. There were still several houses left in the ghetto. In spite of their tanks and their bombs, they hadn't been able to wipe out everything. We had come there to finish the job. When we'd enter a house, we always found a few dead bodies, mostly decomposing corpses, people who had been asphyxiated. We would take them out. And then we went back to Jaworzno.

He will say nothing more about Warsaw. And I won't ask him anything else. Here you have it: houses, corpses, ruins. What more do you want to know? Once you are told "death," what question can you still ask? To know what it's like to trample in death, to slosh around in blood, to lug corpses all day long, to constantly breathe in the air of death? To know what it's like to live for months, for years, submerged in a bath of death, and TO NOT DIE YOURSELF? TO SURVIVE THAT? Basically, that's what you want to know. But you know nothing.

Back at the Jaworzno mine, Avrum's new boss is a Pole, a Pole from the very city of Jaworzno. His name was Szupek. Szupek was his name, Avrum repeats, as though he were fond of the name. Szupek was not an anti-Semite. Sometimes he would bring a piece of bread to the bottom of the mine for Avrum, and even a little bit of lard. Every day he'd say to him, "*Zydku*, Jew, today we'll carry one kilo less coal. We're not here to be worked to death . . ." This Szupek, on top of not being an anti-Semite, was also not a fool.

○

Fanny was ready to spend the night there, huddled in this doorway, waiting for daylight. But then she made up her mind, after all, to go in search of a hotel. She went out in the snow. And who then does she see coming toward her, a militia man in black? No, the son of the butcher on rue Bisson, Aby Dawidowicz, Ginette's big brother. A miracle. He had a "hideout," and Fanny followed him. And when they came into the room, and Aby removed his trenchcoat, the machine gun that jumped out at her seemed to Fanny larger than herself. On top of that, he had around his waist what seemed like a complete arsenal of grenades and cartridges.

Aby lit a fire. Fanny changed her baby. And they went to bed.

Aby was on a mission. His FTP detachment "ran" the Grenoble-Lyon line. Aby was to locate the right places. In the early morning they'd take the streetcar from downtown Grenoble to the Sassenage terminus, going the rest of the way on foot, at night, until they got to Voreppe. They would arrive at midnight, and a train was scheduled to come through at twelve thirty. Armed with a steel bar, they'd lever up the railroad tracks once they removed the bolts holding them in place. Two volunteers remained near the embankment as the rest of the group withdrew. Then, Aby went on, you could hear the sound of the on-coming train, then see the light and the smoke; you could make out the sparks rising from the chimney. First the locomotive would derail, lying down like a wounded animal. Next, the car wagons crashed into each other with an enormous, terrifying racket. Only then did the two volunteers rejoin the rest of the group. They would wait until dawn, when the first streetcar left from Sassenage for Grenoble. They'd return around seven in the morning and go to bed.

During the night Fanny heard a man sobbing. Aby had learned the day before that Ginette, his little sister, had been deported.

O

Avrum's story:

One night, after we came up from the mine, we were forced to leave. We had to walk 190 kilometers, from Jaworzno to Blechhammer. It was the death march, says Toba. There were four or five thousand of us at the beginning. Two mornings later, only half of us reached the front gate of Blechhammer. It was still night. They counted us. I fainted. I arrived at Blechhammer more dead than alive. I couldn't even tell if my heart was still beating. We had walked for two days and two nights, stopping now and then in sheds along the way to Gleiwitz. Whoever fell down was shot in the head. It was the death march, says Toba. Arriving in Blechhammer, in the barracks, I climbed onto one of those beds covered with sawdust and a straw mattress. With all the strength I had left I pulled two of those mattresses on top of me, over my head—I probably weighed about seventy pounds— and when I came to, underneath those two mattresses, I heard a frightening din throughout the entire block. I looked around. Everyone was running. I climbed off the bed, elbowed my way through. Some guys had snatched a bag of powdered sugar, I don't know how or where, and they poured some into the palms of my hands. I went back to bed and began to lick the sugar. Then I dove back under the mattresses and stayed under until the next day. The state I was in, what would happen would happen. When I woke up, there was a great calm in the camp. You could have heard a pin drop. Outside the barracks, dozen of corpses. Some people had gone out, to find better cover. The cold and the fatigue had killed them. A dead body, among us, was nothing. A dead man was zero. Every day we would tell ourselves, if I were dead I would be happy. And then we heard shells exploding. And then Germans came into the camp. There were no SS among them. They wanted to kill us all. They screamed, "*Alles raus*," everyone out. The Russians were next door. Those who went out were killed. We found them a little later, shot, on a wooden slope by a railroad track. Lined up all in order, by rank and file, drenched in blood. The Russians entered the camp on January 25, 1945.

On that day, in France, Grenoble had been long since liberated. Charles is back with Fanny. In Sassenage, it's a holiday. Esther is not yet a year old.

Charles got to Paris that August ahead of Fanny. He arrived at night at the Gare de Lyon. Since there was no public transportation, he reached Belleville on foot, went up Oberkampf Street, walked along Belleville Boulevard, passed by rue des Couronnes, arriving at rue Lesage where Fanny's father, Szymon Tenenbaum, lived.

Charles was wearing heavy, studded German army boots. The sound of his own footsteps hammering the road made him afraid. He thought of himself—he didn't know why—as a German, and he couldn't get the rhythm of an SS slogan out of his head: "Hard as Krupp steel, hard as Krupp steel . . ."

Years later, each time he heard Charles Trenet sing *Retour à Paris,*

> *Revoir Paris*
> *Et me retrouver chez moi*
> *Seul sous la pluie*
> *Parmi la foule des grands boulevards**

he would experience intact the emotion he felt on that morning when he was back in Paris, soon after the liberation. But alone.

Charles met Fanny's father, who was occupying his brother Avrum's apartment. He had had no news of him since his letter from Drancy. Szymon Tenenbaum was happy to see him, anxious to see his daughter again and little Esther. This happened at dawn one November day in 1944.

O

Uncle Avrum didn't notice the Soviet soldiers surround the camp until January 24, 1945. He was taken to a small town, Grosswalden, and cared for in a church. Then a Russian truck drove him to Gleiwitz, where the bakers were required to provide bread to any deportee who showed up. Then Katowice, departure point for a long trip to Odessa, in cattle cars. The Soviets gave him some denims to replace his "pajamas." He left Odessa on the

---

*To see Paris again, and find myself back home, alone in the rain, amid the crowds on the boulevards.

first of May, at night. He spent twelve days at sea on the *Monoway*, an Australian ship.

Avrum reached Marseille on May 12, 1945. Too exhausted to take the train to Paris and reach the Hotel Lutétia with the others, he turned up at the Gare de Lyon two days later in work clothes but without shoes: his feet were wrapped in paper. He took the metro. He weighed seventy-five pounds. It was May 15, 1945.

○

Charles's story:

In the streets, when I would recognize old friends back from the camps, wearing their deportee jackets, head shaved, I would say hello from a distance, not daring to come close. I avoided talking to mothers whose sons hadn't come back or had been shot. People would say— and I can still hear them—"You see, they didn't all die. Some of them managed to come back." And then, and then I met a Jew from Warsaw who knew my mother. He was also from Nowolipie, and I think that he lived in the building where the grocery store had been. He had taken refuge in Russia during the war and came back to Warsaw in 1945. And he'd met Jews who stayed hidden in the Aryan Zone during the German occupation. Someone spoke to him about my mother. She had managed very well, he was told. She'd been terrific. She took in sick people, people with typhus. She'd hide them in our house, bring them food. Everyone in the ghetto worshipped her. There's even a rumor that a book was written about her. But I never found that book. Maybe it's not true. Or maybe there is such a book somewhere, in a Warsaw library. Or in Jerusalem. Or in New York. She was very brave. Too brave. Right before the liquidation of the ghetto, suddenly, she had enough. She had gone through so much, such misery, that she turned herself in to the Germans. She must have suffered so much, seen so much grief at home, all around her, that she asked them to kill her. She couldn't take it anymore. She became hysterical. They didn't say no. They never said no to that. They must have led her to the *Umschlagplatz*. Probably she was gassed right away in Treblinka II.

A pause.

Nathan, my oldest brother, had gone over to the Soviet side during the occupation. He told my mother to come along. If she would go, the rest of the family would follow. But she was a real *yidishe mame* and said: "What? And leave all this, the house, the *betgevant*, the bedding. . . . I have time: I'll sell it all and then I'll come . . ." And she would promise, always promise, and then it was too late, for her and everyone else.

Bolek was engaged to a girl from Vilna. When the Germans came, he went to be with her. They were both deported.

My sister Guta decided one day, finally, to go join Nathan in the USSR. She left her husband in Warsaw, because Misha Peltzman was still waiting for a better time to leave. She paid someone to cross the demarcation line and arrived at Grodno. But the Germans were faster. It's from Grodno that she was deported. She had just enough time to entrust her little girl to a Polish doctor, who kept her throughout the war. Today this niece lives in Israel. She's the only one, along with Nathan, who survived.

Before the war, Nathan had made a sculpture, the *Tennis Player*. It was supposed to be shown at the Olympic Games in Berlin in 1936. But he refused. This sculpture stayed in our home, in our room. It was hollow on the inside, so when the war broke out, my mother hid provisions in it. That's what Nathan told me when I saw him again. He went back to Warsaw after the war, to his comrades in *Hashomer Hatzair*. He had changed his looks in the Soviet Union. "How, during the war, did you give yourself an *arishn punim*, an Aryan face?" people would ask. It's a play on words with *narishn punim*, a stupid face.

A pause.

They're all dead. My mother in Warsaw (my father died before the war). Bolek in Vilna. My sister in Grodno. My brother-in-law, Misha Peltzman, in Warsaw. Only Nathan is left, now in New York. And a niece in Israel.

A pause.

When Nathan went back to Warsaw, he was with two other Jews. They had made up their minds to see their homes once more. Nathan went to Nowolipie. Everything had been razed. There was *nothing* left.

Nothing.

It was an open field.

Next to where our house had been, in Nowolipie, there was a bazaar. One of the Jews with Nathan saw something hanging from a hook, protruding from part of a ruin, something like a sign. "I think that might be it. I think that this is the place where you lived . . ."

A pause.

After the war I realized that I'd lost my parents. I woke up every night. They were murdered, they were murdered, I would tell myself. I didn't understand. I couldn't understand how someone could be eliminated just because he was Jewish. Why? I asked myself—they didn't walk on all fours. They were poor, true, but not harmful. Even today, I don't understand. It's beyond me. My mind blocks.

A pause.

I was twenty-five years old when the war ended. I was old. And since then I've been told that for many other people it was much more tragic. For me it's tragic enough. It will do. What else do you want to know? You can't do anything to make the past come back, to have what happened not happen.

A pause.

My mother used to say to me: I have only one wish in life, it's to live long enough to know how you'll turn out. That's my dream. Because you are my little *muzhinkl*, my youngest. She always said to me . . .

O

Fanny and Charles waited for Rivka and Esther to return. Esther-Rose grew up in this waiting. She must have participated in this waiting. Instead of plugging the gap, soothing, or embodying its deceptiveness, its delusion, she became, through her name only, the very palpable, visible, loud presence of that absence.

After the war, the birth of Mathieu extended the family circle. The family circle enlarged the hole in the middle. The family circle described the circumference of a hole. A hole that nothing, not even time, could fill. Not Yanick's birth. Not Esther's marriage to Simon P. Not Mathieu's to Véronique Piquet. Not Julien's birth. The greater the size of the circle, the larger the hole in the middle. One day it would become vast as the sea. Then perhaps it would no longer be visible, it would be so vast. Perhaps, thinks Mathieu, Esther killed herself to prevent the circle from enlarging, so that the perimeter of the hole would recede, so that we wouldn't forget that there was, there still is, a hole. So that we wouldn't forget that we all came from that hole, from that sea of ashes. That a whole generation of Jews was born of that hole, that sea. That this generation, unlike the others, had to learn or relearn how to breathe. How to stand ground, how to hold on to the ground, to the edge of the ground as to the edge of a pit, feet dangling above piles of naked, crushed, still bleeding corpses.

3

The summer before our separation, Esther took off for
New York. She had been dreaming about it for years.
She used to call me from there. Collect. Which bothered
me, it's expensive you know. And to tell me what? That
she wanted us to separate. Given that already I wasn't
too happy about her calling me collect from New York, I
wasn't too eager to prolong the conversation. And on top
of it all, to hear her say what? So I kept quiet. I was
dumbfounded. Yes, I was, yet I told her: Okay, let's separate. Then she kept quiet. And I didn't say anything
either. Rather expensive, this silence. This silence was
costing a pretty penny. Perhaps she would have wanted
me, yes, I think that must have been it, she wanted me
to protest, to get down on my knees, yes, "on my knees":
no, no, let's stay together, I really want us to, I really
love you, it would be a mistake to separate, I need you,
we still love each other, don't we? I'd never be able to
meet somebody as good as you, never, I'd never do better,
let's try again, go back to zero, start out on a new foot,

get things straight. Let's talk about it, put our cards on the table, see if we can't solve our problems. But, no, I kept quiet. I had had enough. You see, I had had enough. So I didn't say anything. And her trip, her calling, it was all very expensive. Did she go to New York just to call me? She could have called me from Paris, better yet, she could have talked to me directly, at home. Besides, I would have told her the same thing, if she were here, or in New York, or elsewhere, I would have told her: Okay, if you wish, we'll separate. What else could I have told her? Fall on my knees, beg her, implore her? I ask you!

A year earlier, she had fallen in love with a film-maker—it bothers me to tell you this. Well. His name was Jacques Lipshitz. A good-looking guy, it's true. Much better than me. At least, physically. But otherwise, a bastard. He was making a film on the camps; you get the idea. She couldn't stop talking about him, calling him, writing him. She told me everything; she couldn't help it. Note that she wasn't cheating on me, no. Not at all. No, but she had to tell me all about it. To annoy me, perhaps. Or because she couldn't help it. I think it was because she couldn't help it. And then she became more and more unhappy. That she couldn't hide either. Maybe it was the fact that he was making a film on the camps that intoxicated her. But I could also have told her all about the camps. And much better than him, believe me, much better. I could tell her from experience, from the inside out. Because my parents were at Auschwitz and, as you know, were gassed there. I can tell you all there is to know on this subject, I'd tell her. As if I'd been there myself. As if. What do you want to know? You have specific questions? I've read everything there is about it. But even if I hadn't read a thing, it would be the same. So let's have your questions. What's the point of a film about the camps? What sense does it make, a film about the camps? Is it ethnography? A love story in Auschwitz? A documentary? A television special? With celebrities, movie stars? Or else a porno film? I can tell you about it, the porno film on Auschwitz. What more can he say to you, your Lipshitz? I ask you. Auschwitz turns you on? Because it rhymes with Lipshitz? Or just the opposite? I'm asking you. You see, I might not be Dr. Polack, but I understand everything, I used to tell her.

And apparently Jacques Lipshitz paid no attention to her. At least, that's what I came to understand. He probably had women falling all over him. He must have made a big splash at those parties he attended: I'm making a film about Auschwitz. Yes, just think, how it drew people around him, everyone all ears as soon as he dropped that word, everyone crowding around him, trying to touch him, this Lipshitz, a new god, a god for the eighties, perfect for the eighties. Whatever the eighties needed, Lipshitz had it. Esther disappointed me, she really did. Don't think it was because I was jealous. No, only disappointed, really disappointed, greatly disappointed. Infinitely disappointed. You can't know.

He must have felt, Jacques, that with Esther, he would be trapped in a dead-end affair. Because what exactly was she willing to give up? Had she really thought it through? Weighed the pros and cons of taking up with him? Was it yes—yes, or yes—maybe, or yes—let me think about it? That's what her Jacques wanted to know. Even if she told him that she was through with me, that I didn't fulfill her, that I was this and that, too much this, not enough that, basically, she didn't know. She really wasn't ready. In love? Yes. Wanting him? Yes, since she said so. But ready to take the step, right now, tomorrow? She hadn't decided yet. She still needed time to think about it. To think about me. You see, we were like brother and sister. What could I tell her? I ask you. As you wish, I told her. If you want it. What else could I tell her? And she blamed me for not helping her, imagine! What did she expect? That I say to her, Esther, it would give me great pleasure to see you take up with him, really, it would be the most beautiful thing you could do for me. Go ahead, I beg you, don't hesitate. And you'll see, you'll choose on good ground, you'll make the right choice, and I'll accept your choice. I couldn't really say that, could I? A doormat, a *shmatte*, if you wish, and she could wipe her feet on me, but not him too, not both of them. So I told her, if you start anything with him, I'll leave you, so now you know. Well, I wasn't really helping her, I was selfish, a monster of selfishness. And her cries, they would only admit to her guilt. Because she immediately broke into tears. She felt very guilty about me. She had already betrayed me, hadn't she? And she was still very attached to me. All this was beyond her, and me too. I couldn't put myself in her place. And why should I? I'm asking you. Was that perhaps my role? I didn't know anything about this business and, besides, I think neither did she.

And then, one evening, at twilight, very calmly, while we were in bed, I remember it very well, she ended up by saying the words that should not have been spoken, and those words were the last straw; I was ready to hear anything except those words, especially the way she spoke them, calmly, matter-of-factly, as if reaching a conclusion. She said: You see, Simon, I don't love you anymore, I don't love you anymore, that's it, Simon. And I was ready to hear anything, even that; I'd heard so much, we told each other everything, we were like brother and sister. Maybe that's why it wasn't working, because we were like brother and sister, we were like one. You shouldn't be like brother and sister, it's not good, it's fatal. In the end, you can't breathe. I hope that it's not like that for you and Véronique. Well, even that, I don't love you anymore, I was ready to hear it, I was ready for anything. At least, that's what I thought. Because it turned out that I just couldn't take it. But it's only during the next few days that I realized that I couldn't take it, that I couldn't swallow that—it left me with a bitter taste, an aftertaste that's still there, maybe. No, at the time, all I said to her, repeated to her, was: As you wish, Esther, if you wish. You choose, Esther. Then she cried, and cried. But I had had enough. Deep down, I knew that I shouldn't have answered her with "as you wish, if you wish." That I should have protested, cried, passed out, who knows? Now looking back, I know one thing, see, that I answered her like that because that's what I really thought, at that moment, I really didn't care if she left me, if we separated. She could say whatever she liked, I'd agree completely, whatever her decision. So that in making her choice, in deciding, she would decide for me. I don't love you anymore, let's separate, maybe those were the very words I wanted to say. The words I wouldn't dare to utter, and therefore left her with the responsibility to say. Because I didn't have the courage myself. But, in fact, she said nothing. She simply stated her wish to go to New York. Why New York, you ask. Why not New York? She had her reasons, and it didn't matter to me, it really didn't. I had had enough. I want to get my bearings, she said. Fine, go get your bearings, I told her, go to New York.

Jealous of the filmmaker? No, not at all. Why should I have been jealous? I was convinced that she'd never go with him, never. I didn't have to lose sleep over it. Because to take up with him meant she would have to decide, she would have to be the one who broke up. And of that she wasn't capable, even though one of her friends, Anna Krawetz, urged her to do it. But advice is cheap. I wasn't capable either, capable of saying: Look, I packed my bags, I'm leaving tomorrow. I rented a hotel room. Incapable of saying it, because I was incapable of doing it. Can you see me, all alone in a hotel room, alone like a dog? She was the only one I had in the world, you see. I no longer have my parents. Really, only her in the whole world. And, then, Lipshitz didn't want her. Not his type, I suspect. Too good for him, really. You see everything was checkmate. We lived like this for six months. I took refuge in my work at the university. She took refuge in nothing. She couldn't write anymore, could do nothing anymore. I no longer felt like touching her. She had become, for me, not quite like a stranger, but like a sister, see, a sister who has problems but for whom you can't really do much—you can't really do much.

And Auschwitz? No, Auschwitz, not at all, absolutely no connection. Why?

One day, to liven things up a bit, we had some people over. I invited my thesis director and his wife, who was of German origin. He was a rather talkative man, all in all, a pleasant, easygoing conversationalist. At one point he was complaining about the time it took for them to reach the top of Rocamadour when they were traveling with their children last year. Very simple, he said, in front of us there were three busloads of Germans. Then everyone nodded, and Esther remarked: Add a bunch of Ukrainians, and you'll have Auschwitz. No one understood, except me. I laughed nervously . . .

I knew that she really didn't love Lipshitz. It wasn't possible. In spite of everything, I knew her well, your sister. She couldn't have loved somebody like him. Except out of madness, sheer madness.

And, besides, the previous year, things had gone badly for her at the *lycée*. She couldn't stand teaching anymore. Or working, period. She wanted to write, write a novel, something she had set her heart on for a long time, forever it seemed. Because she spoke about it the first day I met her. She never wanted to show me a single page and I respected her privacy. It's premature, she would say. I didn't insist. She showed Lipshitz, though. For him it wasn't premature. She wanted to seduce him. Me, she didn't have to seduce. It was done, you see. I loved her because she was who she was. It's Montaigne who said this, no? She always criticized me for not being literary enough . . . So I suggested she stop working for a while, ask for a leave. Take a year off, then she would see. I earned enough for both of us. And her leave went very badly. Even worse than when she was teaching. She sank. She fell in love. She reproached me: I didn't listen to her enough, not really. I gave her bad advice. I'm the one who pushed her to get her master's degree. Bad advice. And to take a leave, the first in the seven years she'd been teaching. Bad advice. I encouraged her to keep on writing each time she reached the point of giving up. Bad advice. Our relationship became very burdensome.

When she went to New York, in July 1974, I learned what it's like to be carefree. Almost for the first time in my life. An unbelievable feeling of freedom, of well-being. I was finishing my dissertation. I never worked so well. The house was so calm. We'd never been separated before. Like two orphans, two little sparrows frightened of the world, of people. We always stuck together. The two of us were one. Siamese twins. Finally, she's the one who had the courage. She's the one who left. Or, rather, she's

the one who gave me, as though on purpose, as though
by elaborate design—a reason to leave her. Because she
didn't take action. She was content to say, one evening,
Simon, I don't love you anymore, I'm going to New York
to get my bearings. What did that mean? What did she
expect when she returned? A new honeymoon? No, yet
during her absence I got along very well. I noticed that
I lived very well without her. That I was a *mensch*, a
person, even without her. And then I met Betty. A totally
different woman. Not Jewish, like your Véronique.

Auschwitz? I don't really see . . . It's true that novel
she wanted to write revolved around that, the deportations. I think she never wrote a single line of it. Or perhaps just a few fragments. Which she showed only to
Lipshitz. Note that I didn't hold that against her. I really
understood why she didn't show me any of it, especially
me. Because of my parents. She was ashamed to be writing about that. Ashamed in relation to me. Precisely because of my parents. She had thought a lot about the
German camps. Much more than me. For me, my parents
were enough. No need for further reflection. They were
gone, they were gone, what more do you want? I thought
about it enough when I was a child. I upset her once by
saying that she'd never master her subject, which is why
she couldn't write her book. It's true, it irritated me,
that she wanted to write about that. I really didn't want
her to tell me about it. She never showed me her writing
because, basically, I never asked her. I didn't want to
read it. But she spoke the truth, after all, in saying that
it was the only subject that couldn't be mastered. By that
she meant that it was the only subject that was worthwhile. She couldn't have written about anything else. She
wanted to place an epigraph in her book, a quote from
Kierkegaard, wait . . . "Written."/ "For whom?" / "Writ-

ten for the dead, for those you loved in the past." / "Will they then read me?" / "No."

When she was a child, she was afraid that they were coming to get her, that the Nazis would come and get her. She had nightmares every night. For a while she insisted on sleeping curled-up on the floor, by the front door. She would sleep only there, by the front door. Don't you remember? She didn't tell you about it?

For a while, she wanted to write a fictionalized biography of the Yiddish poet Itzhak Katzenelson. Have you ever heard of him? No? He had a strange destiny. Well, strange isn't exactly the word . . . He was in the Warsaw Ghetto, and thanks to a counterfeit passport, a South American passport, was able to get out with his son, before the Ghetto was liquidated. He arrived in France and was interned in the Vittel camp. Toward the end of 1944, he was deported to Auschwitz. Several months after the war, they found three bottles buried near a tree in the Vittel camp. It was the manuscript of a long poem he wrote, *The Song of the Assassinated Jewish People*. It was translated into French. In it he speaks of Mila Street filled with fear, of the selections; he says that the Germans remained on the sidelines, looking on from a distance, not meddling in. It was with Jewish hands that the Germans killed the Jews, he said. And that's really the great mystery, isn't it? That's what you cannot explain. They'll say what they will, the historians, theologians, philosophers, but they'll never explain it. It's like God . . .

For me, meeting a non-Jew was very important. I was crossing something out, turning a new page. With Esther, you couldn't turn a new page. The past was eating us alive. It's not a question of forgetting, you know. How could I ever forget my parents? No, it was simply a question of turning a new page, of going on with life.

In New York she had an affair with a taxi driver, a Jew, older than her. She told me about it. It was the first time in twelve years of marriage that she was unfaithful. Her telling me about it had no effect on me. A stranger she would never see again, living at the other end of the world . . . She met him the day she arrived; he was the first person to whom she said a word. It happened in July of 1974; it was very hot, the man was in shirtsleeves. He had a blue number tattooed on his arm. And just as she was going to tell him where she wanted to go, suddenly she found that she couldn't speak, at least not in English. So she spoke to him in Yiddish. He was very surprised to hear her speak that language. Well, in brief, they made a date to meet the next day in Central Park. He took her to his place right away. As for me, I had done the same thing that July 1974. I had met Betty in my lab. She had come to do a report on the effect of new government guidelines on current research. Later, after our separation in the fall of 1974, Esther reproached me for abandoning her, called me a bastard. Maybe I was a bastard, as she said. But I don't think so. . . . She was getting worse and worse, your sister. I kept telling her on the telephone that all I wanted was for her to be happy. Was she capable of wishing me the same? I doubt it. She needed help. And she wanted no other doctor but me. She would tell me: But didn't I help you, all that time you were writing your thesis? A joke, I thought . . .

In the months preceding her decision to go to New York, I suggested that we visit Poland. I wanted to see the country, the former Jewish villages, the old Jewish quarters in the big cities, and, above all else, the Ghetto. Or, rather, where it had been. And then, maybe, if I had the courage, I wanted to see Auschwitz, to see where my parents died. This project repelled her. And she spoke about it to this Lydia Polack she was seeing three times a week. She told her about her revulsion. According to Lydia Polack, Esther's reluctance to go to Poland was related to the difficulty she had in speaking about her childhood and the past, especially to her, Lydia Polack. Because of her name, Polack, you see. . . . In spite of it all, there was an objective reason for her refusing to go to Poland. In her imagination, that country represented the largest Jewish cemetery that ever existed. Not even a cemetery. A land of ashes, as she said. The land of Jewish ashes. And, then, I think that there was yet another, more complicated reason, which was that I was the one who had suggested we go, I was the one who wanted to go. She said that she wasn't ready to go there, that first she had to write her book. As for the homology between Poland and Polack, obviously . . .

One day, sitting on Lydia's couch, she noticed an ink drawing on the wall in front of her. It showed a train station, people carrying suitcases. This drawing had always been there, in that same place, but for the first time Esther noticed it. But it's terrible, she said, that's exactly the kind of drawing that I'm doing—train stations, disheveled people with suitcases. And Lydia Polack told her that the parents of the artist who did this drawing that hung on the wall next to the couch in her office— placed there on purpose for her patients to notice or not notice, which was just as interesting—anyway, they had been deported. And Esther told her about Jacques Lipshitz with whom she had fallen in love. She even confessed that she began to love him passionately, madly, the day he told her he was getting ready to shoot a film about the camps. That's what overwhelmed her. . . . She told me everything. She wrote me crazy things from New York. Europe stinks of gas, she said. This smell hadn't crossed the Atlantic. All of Europe is covered with the ashes of Auschwitz. Those were the kinds of things she would write me.

You know, the first time we went to the movies together, your sister and I, it was to see Resnais' *Night and Fog.* Our relationship began under strange auspices, you see . . .

She often dreamed of dogs. Always German Shepherds, who would bite her. What did Lydia Polack say about that? I don't know. . . . You know this story that Jews tell? Whenever I see a German Shepherd in the street, I always wonder what his grandfather was doing during the war . . .

When I knew Esther, I think, she didn't love me. She wasn't in love with me. She probably respected me, maybe even admired me, but love, no . . .

What else do you want to know? I don't feel guilty about . . . about . . .

Speaking of dog dreams, Lydia Polack allegedly explained to her that when Esther was a child she wanted to have children; and later to have children seemed repugnant to her, even frightening. Which explains how love, for her, was transformed into the fear of dogs. At least that's how I understood it. Now, why German, why German Shepherds? . . . But it's a fact that she didn't want children. She wanted to write a book. For her, it was either children or books.

Why "German," why "German Shepherds"?

You know that your Aunt Esther was deported with your grandmother Rivka in July of 1942, like my parents. And this Aunt Esther, your mother's sister, was only twenty years old then. She didn't have children. And Esther, your sister, because she had the same name as your aunt, sometimes felt as if she had taken her place, her

life, in some way. This she was able to discover with Lydia
Polack. Because in questioning Fanny, she learned that
it was Fanny who was on the cops' list for the roundup.
And Fanny who went to hide with *goyishe* neighbors. The
cops took away the two women, your grandmother and
your aunt. Of the grandmother, Esther never spoke. It
was the aunt, only the aunt, who haunted her. Because
of the name, I think. And then, as a little girl, she thought
of herself a bit as the daughter of her grandfather, Szymon, who had lost his oldest child, Esther.

After the war, whenever he had a free moment, he
would come for her and take her out. They spoke Yiddish
together . . . She talked a lot about him, Szymon Tenenbaum. That's how she'd refer to him. She never said my
grandfather. She'd say Szymon Tenenbaum, pro-
nouncing it *Shimone*. Odd, isn't it, that she'd hit on somebody with exactly the same first name . . . When they
went out walking together, as soon as he heard anyone
speaking German—in the street, in a café—it seemed he
would approach and speak to him, give him directions,
ask him what town he came from. He couldn't help it,
and Esther never asked why he did that. But she was
proud that her grandfather spoke German to a German.
Perhaps she was proud that he spoke a real foreign language, a language other than Yiddish or French. Those
languages, they were ordinary. Everybody spoke them.
She told me that she used to beg Szymon to take her with
him to Germany, to show her the country whose language
he spoke. And don't forget that her aunt Esther was born
in Germany, in Düsseldorf, I think; they were en route
to France. It all leads me to believe that your sister
wanted to replace, thought she was replacing, her grandfather's older daughter. She herself was the eldest in your

family . . . And, besides, she had the same first name. Maybe she wanted to die like her.

Esther had just turned twenty when the two of us went to Germany. Hitch-hiked. It was in 1963. One night we came to Düsseldorf. We weren't at all thinking about those stories, or any of that business. At least, we hadn't mentioned it. The German truck driver who had given us a ride asked us where we wanted him to drop us off. And Esther made an awful slip of the tongue. She said *Judenherbergen* instead of *Jugendherbergen*. Jewish Hostel instead of Youth Hostel . . . awful, isn't it. I could have died.

When your sister was seeing this Lydia Polack, she used to write down all her dreams so that she could discuss them with her. I remember a dream that she told me over the phone—we spoke only on the phone then, we were separated. It was a dream about the war. Some German and French women stood facing each other in uniform. Each one of them pointed her gun—a real gun—but with a child's dart inserted in the barrel. The dart of the German woman-soldier facing her was held firmly in place; it could hit its mark. Esther's dart, on the other hand, hung loose in the gun barrel; it was useless. The German fired, and the rubber tip of her dart reached the tip of Esther's gun and stuck to it. Then everything blew up. They were all killed. Esther woke up with a start. She remembered that your Uncle Avrum, Szymon's brother, had once given her such a dart-gun. An odd gift for a little girl. But, as you know, Avrum had returned from Auschwitz. Esther was convinced that the German woman who faced her in this dream was the one she called "the real Esther," meaning her aunt who was born in Germany and killed in Auschwitz. She said that in the dream the "real" Esther killed the false Esther, that is, herself, your sister. Your sister, therefore, was the false Esther. Everybody thought she was real, but she alone knew the truth, that she was a fake, that she was usurping another's place, her identity. Her life! The place, the identity, the life of the other woman. The real one had given her place to the fake. Maybe that's why your sister had always thought she was dead, or, at least, that she was forbidden to live. In her mind, she had created an entire book about it. A book about Treblinka, the Warsaw Ghetto, all of it. Because of the other grandmother, Raisl, I think, right? Don't forget that Esther's middle name was Rose. She was named after two women she had never known, two women who disappeared without a trace . . . like my parents . . .

Did she leave a manuscript? No, I didn't find anything. Perhaps she destroyed it? Or perhaps there never was one, how can you know? What did she show Lipshitz? It was nothing, I think, only a few pages. Nothing really.

If I feel guilty? Yes, I feel guilty. How could I not feel guilty? Who, in my place, would not feel guilty? I ask you. I'm ten years older than you. I learned one thing: in life, sometimes it's either you or the other person. I'm not saying it's always like that; I'm saying it's sometimes like that. There comes a time when you have to choose: you or the other person. And, sometimes, if you don't choose, either because you lack the courage or the cruelty to choose, then it's both of you, both you and the other, whom you, out of weakness, allow to die, to cave in to death. Courage, cruelty, or, if you prefer, self-preservation—or call it love of life—demands that you choose. Choose to live. I chose. I chose life. If choosing life means being guilty, then, yes, I'm guilty. It's written in the Torah: Choose life . . .

If it takes the other person's death? . . . It just so happens that the Germans have a saying, "one person's death is another person's bread." *Der einer Tod ist der anderen Brot.* In the death camps, in Poland, the night before a convoy was due to arrive, the prisoners who hadn't been gassed yet would noisily rejoice. Especially if they learned that the convoy was coming from Western Europe, from Holland, or Belgium. Because those would be rich Jews who were coming. With food, and gold, and diamonds. And in the blocks they would rejoice. They knew that with all those Jews about to be gassed, they themselves could hold out a few more days. And when the convoy was made up of Jews from Poland, from Galicia or Lithuania, then they were desperate. Because those Jews would come with nothing. *Der einer Tod ist der anderen Brot.*

Have I become a Nazi? . . . I was wrong, after all, to tell you all this, you couldn't understand. You were born after the war.

That's it. Yesterday I could finally tell Véronique that, because of Jacqueline Roubestan's recommendation to her supervisor, I was being promoted to assistant director of administration. For now, I accepted this event willingly. Even better, I was happy about it. Véronique and I immediately decided to have a second child, right then and there, that very night. Maybe we managed to do it. Our son Julien was born somewhat by chance. We had just gotten married, we didn't really, consciously, wish for his arrival. Now we wanted another child. We would know how to expect it, really expect it. By the time that he's born I'll have finished with Esther, that phantom. With the past. That particular past. Simon is right: you had to turn over a new leaf. For me, that day is near. With the last page of my book I'll turn the page on my past, the long gone past. And if I still haven't quite understood the reason—the real, ultimate reason—for my sister's suicide, in any case I have the will to turn my back on it forever. My child will be spared the past. He won't carry its stigma. He'll really be an *afterward* child. Standing between him and the war would be a new generation, an interval of space that could protect him as from a horrible taint. Never will I talk to him about Esther. Her name will be dead. My book will have blotted her out. Oddly enough, you need words for that. Words, and not silence. Only words can do that, erase her memory, just as the confession of a crime, they say, brings the criminal a semblance of peace. And here I go again, speaking of crimes. . . But my wish to have a child, a second child, at least proves to me that my "sin" has dropped away as if it were a foreign body, a tooth, a dead branch, rotten fruit fallen from the tree, whatever. Esther is buried—well and good. Her grave is in full view somewhere in the Bagneux cemetery. Her name is on the tomb, and her body below. Localized. Esther is no longer in me. I've ejected her, and know how to keep her at a distance forever. And when she'll come too close, I'll be careful, never allow her to reach me: I'll know how to push her away. I'll have to. All I need to do is look at my child to know that I must. My child must live, not simply survive. It's my duty as a father to allow him this life to which he's entitled. No direct line from Esther to this child. Except maybe through this book. But only a book, nothing more. And if someday he asks me who this Esther was, this sister I'm talking about, I'll tell him that I never had a sister. I had a little brother, his uncle Yanick. Or I'll tell him something else. I'll find something to tell him. I'll tell him, yes, it's true, I had a sister. She died in an auto accident. That's life. In life there is also death. It's a part of it.